"I can't get to sleep," Dizzy said wearily

She was down in Zach's kitchen in the middle of the night heating some milk when Zach came upon her.

"Possibly," he said in frosty disapproval, "it's the unusual occurrence of your sleeping *alone* that's causing the disturbance."

If he didn't so obviously mean every word he said, it might have been funny. But in fact she was the original virgin, hadn't even been kissed properly in her twenty-one years.

"You're probably right," she snapped. "Perhaps you would like to rectify that?"

His mouth twisted. "I don't believe so, thank you," he said with clear distaste.

"Why not? Aren't I good enough for you?"

"I'm sure you are," he drawled, and there was something in his eyes that belied his next words. "Fortunately I'm not attracted to overexperienced children!"

CAROLE MORTIMER, one of our most popular—and prolific—English authors, began writing in the Harlequin Presents series in 1979. She now has more than forty top-selling romances to her credit and shows no signs whatever of running out of plot ideas. She writes strong traditional romances with a distinctly modern appeal, and her winning way with characters and romantic plot twists has earned her an enthusiastic audience worldwide.

Books by Carole Mortimer

HARLEQUIN PRESENTS

HARLEQUIN SIGNATURE EDITION

CAROLE MORTIMER

one chance at love

Harlequin Books

TORONTO • NEW YORK • LONDON
AMSTERDAM • PARIS • SYDNEY • HAMBURG
STOCKHOLM • ATHENS • TOKYO • MILAN

For, John
Matthew and Joshua

Harlequin Presents first edition October 1988
ISBN 0-373-11117-7

Original hardcover edition published in 1988
by Mills & Boon Limited

CHAPTER ONE

'I'M GOING insane! If something doesn't soon happen to free me from here, they're going to have to lock me up in a real prison for killing my own uncle!'

Dizzy held the receiver away from her ear as her friend's voice rose in desperation. 'Do I take it, Christi, dear,' she drawled during a brief respite in the tirade—probably so that Christi could take air into her starved lungs, for she hadn't stopped bemoaning her fate since Dizzy answered her call five minutes earlier, 'that this visit with your uncle isn't working out?' She again held the receiver away from her poor abused ear, as Christi told her exactly what she thought of her visit to the Lake District. 'And I didn't even realise you knew words like that!' she mocked teasingly.

'I mean it, Dizzy,' Christi said frantically. 'I can't stand it here much longer without breaking out in some way that's going to totally destroy any chance of my uncle agreeing to my inheriting my money on my twenty-first birthday!'

Christi always had had a flair for the dramatic, which was perhaps as well, since she had chosen acting as a career, Dizzy acknowledged ruefully. But she very much doubted Christi really would do anything desperate, not when so much depended on her remaining her usually serene self. In fact, this Zachariah Bennett must be a bit of a monster to have ruffled Christi's feathers at all!

'You only have another month to go,' she reminded her friend gently.

'Three weeks and five days,' Christi corrected sharply. 'I've been counting! And I could have murdered him, disposed of the body, and disappeared without trace by then!'

Dizzy couldn't help but chuckle at this uncharacteristic violence from a woman who usually avoided stepping on an ant where possible!

For the last week Christi had been staying with her uncle in his Lake District home, intent on impressing the man who had the guardianship of her inheritance with her maturity and ability to handle the considerable amount of money her parents had left in trust for her on their deaths three years ago. Christi was all too aware that if her uncle decided otherwise she would have to wait until she was twenty-five, when the money would come to her automatically. Dizzy could quite see that murdering her uncle and burying him in an unmarked grave could jeopardise that good impression Christi was trying to make!

'What's wrong with him?' She frowned her puzzlement.

'He's fusty, dusty, spends all day working on history books that no one's going to read——'

'Oh I don't know about that,' Dizzy objected mildly. 'I found his book on the Romans very interesting——'

'I don't consider you any judge of literature when you can spend half an hour looking at a children's annual!' Christi dismissed disgustedly.

And enjoyed every minute of it, too, Dizzy thought with a mischievous grin. But she knew Christi wouldn't appreciate hearing about that in her present mood. 'I was just making sure it was a suitable present for a five-year-old,' she defended without rancour.

'One of your godchildren, I suppose,' her friend sighed acknowledgement. 'How many do you have now?'

'Six,' she related proudly. 'And, in case you're interested, Sarah loved the annual.'

'The only thing I'm interested in at the moment is getting away from here,' Christi groaned. 'When my uncle isn't working, he has his nose stuck in a research book. And Castle Haven is exactly that, Dizzy,' she added incredulously. 'A huge monstrosity of a castle, stuck in the middle of all this water and mountains. It's like being in a giant freezer!' She sounded distraught. 'I never thought I'd be able to sympathise with a joint of beef! I ask you, Dizzy, whoever heard of wearing a jumper in the house in June!'

'A castle, hm?' she repeated interestedly. 'Is it——'

'Dizzy, it's just a draughty old castle!' Christi cut in impatiently. 'It's stuck out in the middle of nowhere, and if my uncle has any friends in the neighbourhood then I haven't met them. Good grief, Dizzy, I actually went to bed at nine-thirty last night. Nine thirty!' she repeated, in case Dizzy hadn't been able to believe it the first time around— as Christi herself obviously hadn't!

And she could quite understand why: Christi was a night person, who didn't usually wake up until ten o'clock in the evening. Things must be more desperate than Dizzy had given Christi credit for!

'How am I going to convince my uncle I'm a responsible adult, perfectly mature enough to handle my own money, if I give in to this craving I have to put my hands around his throat and strangle the life out of him just to relieve the boredom?' Christi wailed emotionally.

This time Dizzy held back her chuckle, trying desperately to appreciate the seriousness of the situation. 'I can see how that might make him have second thoughts,' she finally said, wryly.

'He already thinks I'm irresponsible because I dropped out of college to go to drama school,' Christi told her worriedly.

Dizzy gave a snort of laughter. 'If he thinks you're irresponsible, I hate to think what he would make of me! Christi, why don't you——'

'Oh, damn, the gong just sounded for dinner,' her friend muttered frantically. 'I'll have to go, my uncle "deplores tardiness".' Her change of voice, to stern reproval, over the last two words indicated that it was a direct quote. 'Try and come up with a believable excuse for me to come back to London, Dizzy,' she urged desperately. 'Before I go completely *insane...*'

Dizzy rang off more slowly than her friend, her expression thoughtful as she finished preparing the pilchards on toast that was to be her own dinner. She adored the fish, ate them for breakfast, lunch, and dinner if she had the chance, and indulged the addiction to the full whenever she was alone, which wasn't very often. If having two cats and a dog constantly underfoot could be classed as being alone now! She jealously guarded her dinner as all three animals tried to steal it from her plate as she ate; she really would have to have a word with Christi about the deplorable manners of her pets.

She looked around the flat appreciatively, loving the mellow décor and comfortable furniture, mentally thanking Christi for inviting her to stay and care for her pets for her while she was away. If only Gladys would stop trying to steal her pilchards, she grumbled under her breath, even as she tapped a sneaking paw away from her plate.

Feeling grateful that she wasn't subjected to Christi's enforced early nights, she pulled a tattered and dog-eared book from her capacious shoulder-bag, opening it to the page she had marked half-way through the seven hundred pages, instantly losing herself in the page-turning historical adventure by one of her favourite authors. She had read the book many times before, but Claudia Laurence knew how to write a book so that it was possible to gain something new from it every time it was read. A reader's delight!

Two hundred pages—and five hours—later, Dizzy decided it was time to go to bed. She felt as if she had barely fallen asleep when the telephone beside the bed began to ring, and she shot upright in the bed, completely and suddenly awake. She felt half drunk with tiredness as she picked up the receiver.

'I've got it!' came the eagerly disorientated whisper of a voice.

An obscene telephone call, Dizzy acknowledged disgustedly. 'Well, now that you've got it, you know what you can do with it, don't you?' She reached out to replace the receiver.

'Dizzy!' came the distressed cry down the telephone line, halting her action. 'Dizzy, don't you dare hang up on me!'

She blinked; obscene telephone callers didn't usually know their victims' names, did they? Not that she was an expert on the subject—heaven forbid!—but she didn't think they did. And now that the voice had been raised slightly from that eerie whisper, it did sound vaguely familiar—in fact, it sounded a little like *Christi*. But why on earth would Christi be calling her at—a quarter past six in the morning? she wondered, as she glanced at the bedside clock. Christi hadn't been known to surface before at least eight o'clock before—but then, she had never been known to go to bed at nine-thirty before, either!

Dizzy leant up on her elbow, pushing her long hair back from her face. 'Christi, is that you?' she yawned.

'Of course it's me,' her friend hissed. 'Who else would be calling you at this time of the morning?'

The answer to that was so obvious that Dizzy didn't even attempt to make it. 'Why are you whispering?' she asked curiously, still attempting to clear the fog of sleep from her brain.

'So that no one can hear me!' came the explosive reply.

Logical, she thought as she yawned again, very logical. 'Why don't you want anyone to hear you?' she asked uninterestedly.

'Because it's only six o'clock in the morning!' Christi said exasperatedly, forgetting to whisper, then muttering self-disgustedly as she realised what she had done.

Dizzy ignored the mutterings; she thought it was best to do so. 'Why are you telephoning at six o'clock in the morning if it's going to disturb people?' she urged sleepily, wishing *she* hadn't been one of the people disturbed.

'Because I've come up with a way of getting *me* out of this place!' Christi announced triumphantly.

'Congratulations,' drawled Dizzy drily. 'But couldn't you have waited until a decent hour to let me in on the secret?'

'No—because *you're* going to help get me out!' her friend said with satisfaction.

'You want me to bake you a cake with a metal file in it, and send it to you?' she derided.

Christi groaned at her levity. 'Can't you even be serious when you know what trouble I'm in?'

'Sorry.' Dizzy sobered. 'What do you want me to do that will help you escape from the fusty, dusty Zachariah? Sorry,' she grimaced, as she could sense Christi's rising anger at her teasing. 'Go ahead, you have my full attention,' she encouraged interestedly.

Christi gave a snort that clearly said she doubted that, but she launched into her explanation anyway. 'It was something you said that gave me the idea, actually,' she told Dizzy excitedly, hastily lowering her voice as she realised that, in her enthusiasm, she had once again forgotten to whisper. 'I mean, how can I be considered irresponsible when I'm training for a career, have lived in the same apartment for years, have pets that are well cared for, have——'

'I get the picture—you sober citizen, you,' Dizzy drawled. 'And, as it is now almost six-thirty in the morning, and I've barely had any sleep, do you think you could get to the point?'

'Oh, yes.' Christi gave a dismissive sigh as she realised she had been going on a bit. 'The answer isn't to show my uncle how responsible *I* am——'

'It isn't?' Dizzy frowned; she must have dozed off in the middle of this conversation somewhere, for she had thought Christi's proving to her uncle that she was more than capable of managing her own monetary affairs was exactly the point!

'No,' Christi confirmed impatiently. 'It's showing him how *irresponsible* I'm not!'

From her friend's triumphant tone as she made the announcement, Dizzy knew this was the place she was supposed to come in and tell her how clever she was being, but so far this still didn't make a lot of sense to her.

'Dizzy, you haven't fallen asleep on me, have you?' Christi snapped suspiciously at her prolonged silence.

She roused herself wearily. 'Of course not. And don't shout, you'll wake up the household,' she reminded tiredly.

'It could *do* with waking up,' Christi muttered with feeling.

'We've been through all that,' Dizzy said drily. 'I don't mean to sound unsympathetic, love, but I really can't understand what's so terrible about staying with your uncle for a few weeks. And——'

'You soon will,' her friend said with satisfaction.

'—surely a few early nights aren't going to——

What do you mean, I soon will?' Suddenly, sleep didn't seem so important any more. 'Christi, what are you up to?' she prompted sharply, knowing that whatever it was, she probably wasn't going to like it!

'Who is letting you make free use of her apartment while she's out of town?' Christi prompted calmly.

'Who is baby-sitting your pets—at the cost of pilchards and solitude!—while you are out of town?' she instantly returned.

'Who got up in the middle of the night to open the school dormitory window so that you could climb in off the roof——'

'Who forgot to come down to unlock the door and fell asleep until I climbed up and *knocked* on the window?' she reminded pointedly.

'Oh, all right,' Christi acknowledged impatiently. 'Maybe that was my fault. But who helped get you out of spending the night in prison the time the police raided that illegal gambling——'

'You know very well that I had gone there with a reporter who was doing research for an article,' she protested.

'But who came to the police station and managed to convince the police of that? Who got you away from there before it became public knowledge, and your picture appeared on the front page of all the tabloids?' Christi pounced triumphantly.

'You did,' Dizzy conceded heavily. 'And now I owe you one, right?'

'Oh, no, Dizzy!' Her friend sounded genuinely shocked at the suggestion. 'It isn't a question of paying me back. I was just trying to point out that we're friends, and that friends try to help each other when they can.'

Dizzy gave an indulgent smile, easily able to visualise Christi's earnest expression: that faintly hurt look in enormous blue eyes that dominated the beauty of her face. Christi was tall and elegant, with a natural serenity and kindness; Zachariah Bennett had to be dense not to be able to see that.

Dizzy sighed, freely acknowledging that Christi was the best friend she had ever had. 'What do you want me to do?'

'Come up here and——'

'Not that, Christi,' she protested, visions of being sent to bed at nine-thirty by Christi's ancient uncle flashing through her mind. A truly free spirit, just the thought of it reminded her too much of her childhood.

'—show my uncle just what an irresponsible person is!' Christi finished triumphantly, totally deaf to Dizzy's protest.

'Thanks!' she grimaced ruefully.

'Don't go and act all wounded on me,' her friend chided lightly. 'You've deliberately cultivated your life-style, enjoy having no permanent home, no visible means of support, no real belongings except what you carry about in that cavernous sack you call a shoulder-bag, and the pack you throw on your back.'

'I admit I like to travel light——'

'*Travel* being the operative word,' Christi derided. 'I never knew of anyone wearing out their passport before!'

'I didn't wear it out,' she protested. 'It just got— a little full,' she excused dismissively.

'Exactly,' Christi said with satisfaction. 'You're *everything* that my uncle would consider irresponsible; drifting through life, staying with friends whenever you get the chance——'

'Christi——'

'And God knows *where* you live the rest of the time,' Christi concluded in a starchily disapproving voice—as if she were quoting verse and chapter from a too-familiar sermon.

As indeed she was! Dizzy had heard those very same words from her father too often not to know where they came from. After hearing the same thing for years, she had taken Christi home with her once as self-defence; but even her friend's presence hadn't prevented the usual lecture. Obviously Christi had never forgotten the humiliating experience, either!

'I thought you also called me friend,' Dizzy reminded her drily. 'Although I'm beginning to wonder about that!' she mocked.

'My uncle doesn't have to know that,' Christi dismissed. 'We can say you're just an old school acquaintance of mine who happens to be——'

'Drifting through,' Dizzy finished derisively.

'Exactly,' Christi said eagerly. 'And of course I'm your friend,' she defended indignantly. 'Goodness, *we* know that none of that drivel is true. And, even if it were, it wouldn't make any difference to those of us that love you. You're the most generous, giving, totally unselfish——'

'Enough, enough,' she drawled ruefully. 'When do you want this drifting wastrel of an *acquaintance* to arrive on the castle doorstep, expecting another hand-out?' she prompted drily.

'Today,' Christi pounced eagerly.

Dizzy had been expecting that, otherwise there would have been no need for this hasty call in what was, to her at least, still the middle of the night. 'And who will take care of your food-stealing pets if I leave?' she reminded lightly.

'Lucas will come in from next door and do that,' Christi dismissed. 'They all love him, and he usually does it for me if I go away. And if you hate looking after the cats and dog so much, how come they are always completely spoilt after one of your visits? Last time you came to stay, Gladys and Josephine spent the next week sniffing my food cupboard, looking for your tins of pilchards. And I just bet Henry is sharing your bed right this minute!' she announced disgustedly.

Dizzy looked down guiltily to the foot of the bed, where the Yorkshire terrier was curled up, asleep, on the quilt. 'He gets lonely in the kitchen at night,' she defended. 'And he has such soulful brown eyes that I don't have the heart to say no to him.'

'A pair of soulful brown eyes and loneliness are not reasons to take him into bed with you! He—— Oh, damn, I think I heard someone coming.' Christi lapsed back into that desperate whispering. 'I'll see you later, OK?' she urged frantically, sounding more and more like a hounded animal.

The impression didn't in the least endear the idea of going up to the Lake District to Dizzy, to show herself off as some lost cause just so that Zachariah Bennett could say to Christi, 'Thank God you didn't turn out like *her*, here's your money and welcome to it'!

If it really were going to be as easy as that...

*   *   *

Dizzy had heard much about the beauty of the Lake District, and as her travels usually took her out of the country, rather than around it, this was the first time she had ever seen this lovely part of England.

But nothing she had heard about the Lake District had prepared her for the scenery before her now. No one had told her she could expect to see naked men, one naked man in particular, as he cavorted about in one of the smaller lakes!

As Christi had said, the man in the flat next door to hers had been only too happy to pet-sit Gladys, Josephine and Henry, and so the only hitch there could have been to her setting off for Castle Haven had neatly been removed.

In the clear light of day—after several more hours' sleep—Dizzy was less sure than ever that Christi's plan was a good one. It might work if Zachariah Bennett—the old curmudgeon!—could be made to believe she and Christi *were* just acquaintances, but the two of them had been friends since their first term together at boarding-school over twelve years ago. The familiarity of a friendship like that might be a little difficult to disguise. A telephone call to Christi to tell her just that had elicited the information that her friend had gone out for the morning with her uncle, and so, not knowing what else to do, Dizzy had set out for the castle. They would just have to hope for the best when she got there.

It had been a pleasant trip up on the train. She might be a free spirit, she thought, but she wasn't stupid—it was no longer safe to hitch-hike, if it ever had been! Enquiries at the station, when she got off the train, had told her that the castle was about eight miles away and, after the long train journey, stretching her legs for a few miles sounded like a good idea.

The first six miles of her walk had been really enjoyable—the view of this lake was even more so!

She sat on top of one of the hills that surrounded the lake on all sides, unashamedly watching the sleek-bodied man as he cavorted about in the water like a dolphin. Even water-slicked, his hair was discernible as dark blond, with blond highlights that any woman would envy, but which were obviously perfectly natural on this man. From the deep tan of his body, he swam naked like this often. Old Zachariah Bennett would probably have a seizure if he could see the guest, who was going to soon turn up unexpectedly on his doorstep, watching the antics of this naked man. And enjoying it, too!

He really was a very handsome specimen, she thought admiringly as he stepped out of the water to dry off in the sun. He was tall and lithe, and from the look of him he either cut down trees or built roads for a living, for his muscles had been rippling powerfully. Or else he was just a secret weight-lifter. Whatever he was, a fusty scholar like Zachariah Bennett would probably recoil in horror at such virility: the man's shoulders wide and strong, golden hair glinting on his bronzed chest, his stomach taut and flat, and his hips and thighs... Apollo himself couldn't have looked better!

Dizzy reluctantly drew herself away from the beauty of the scene as the man stretched out in the sun to dry some more. No doubt he wouldn't mind at all that she had been admiring him—he wouldn't have been swimming in a lake where anyone could come along and see him if he did—but she really did have to be getting along to the castle now. It was a pity to spoil the moment, but time was quickly passing, and Christi's thoughts were probably on the unmarked grave again by now!

But she didn't forget the man as she walked the last two miles, whistling happily to herself, the day suddenly seeming full of new possibilities. Maybe the man was a local, maybe Christi would know who he was... But, of course, her friend had said she hadn't met anyone else in the area. What a shame; it might have been interesting meeting the Greek god. It might have helped her irresponsible image along a little more, too, if she could have brought the local womaniser back to the castle to meet the professor.

Not that her image needed any help, she acknowledged ruefully as she glanced down at herself. Her denims were old and patched at the knees, the material faded in the usual places, her T-shirt just as old, but out of shape after numerous washes. She put a self-conscious hand up to the blonde bubbly curls that had escaped the long plait down her spine and that had helped give her her name, framing her small, heart-shaped face that was dominated by green, catlike eyes. Small, just over five feet, with breasts that were slightly too large for her body, and her fly-away blonde hair, she was the perfect 'dizzy blonde' image. No doubt she would be Zachariah Bennett's most unusual house—*castle*—guest, to date!

Castle Haven proved to be exactly what Christi had claimed it was, a huge turreted castle that seemed totally out of place among the placid lakes

and tree-covered hills and mountains that surrounded it on all sides.

Unlike Christi, however, Dizzy found the castle
fascinating, and longed to know its history. But she
supposed that would never do, not when she was
supposed to be showing Zachariah Bennett just how
wayward and uncaring the youth of today could
be, and, in the process, what a shining example of
responsibility his niece was. It would never do to
let old Zach know she was probably as interested
in history as he was!

The castle was a fitting home for him, as a historian of some repute—Dizzy knew him mainly
from his books—and as she drew nearer Dizzy
could see that on the outside, at least, it had been
maintained in beautiful condition. Writing history
books must pay very well! she thought.

The butler who opened the door several minutes
after she had pulled the bell—hoping it was ringing
somewhere in the depths of the castle—looked as
if he might have been here doing this very same
thing since the castle had originally been built!
Snowy-haired, with an aloofness that was felt rather
than physically visible in his thin body and blandly
expressionless face, his disapproval of the 'person'
standing at the huge heavy oak door he had swung
open was a tangible thing. Maybe he was old
Zachariah himself; probably what he earned as a
historian didn't run to a butler as well as a castle!

'Hi!' She gave him her brightest smile, easing her
backpack on to one shoulder. 'My name's Dizzy
James, and I——'

'The castle is not open to the public, Miss James,'
he informed her frostily.

She had been going to say 'I'm a friend of Christi's', but his condescending attitude brought out the devil in her. 'What a pity,' she drawled. 'I'm sure you would get thousands of people wanting to tramp all over the place if you decided to change your mind.' She looked up at him innocently as he stiffened in shock at the suggestion.

His raised eyebrows and pursed lips showed his distaste. 'Let me give you directions back to the main road,' he said coldly. 'You go back the way you just came, and then——'

'Oh, but I don't want to go back to the main road!' She smiled at him, her eyes gleaming like a cat's.

'This is private property, Miss James, and——'

'But I'm here to see Christi Bennett,' she informed him happily.

'Miss Christi?' This time his guard was completely down, due to severe shock and horrified disbelief that 'Miss Christi' could even know such a person!

Obviously, he was the family butler, after all, and as she had only come here to shock Zachariah Bennett, not upset the whole household, she gave the man in front of her her most engaging smile. It had been known to melt frostier hearts than his, although not always, and never when she really willed it to. This time she was partially successful, although only grudgingly, as the butler slowly opened the door for her to come inside.

He nodded to her to wait where she stood, just inside the huge reception area. 'I'll go and tell Miss Christi that you're here——'

'That won't be necessary, Fredericks.' Christi came bounding down the wide stairway like a whirlwind, her face flushed with excitement—the first she had known for some time, by the look of the shadows beneath her usually sparkling blue eyes. 'Dizzy!' she greeted thankfully, clasping her hands in hers before hugging her tightly.

She allowed Christi the indulgence for several seconds, realising her friend was under severe strain. But all the time she was aware of Fredericks as he watched them with distant curiosity, and so she finally whispered to Christi, 'Acquaintances, remember?'

Christi stiffened at the reminder, her arms falling back to her sides as she stepped back reluctantly, forcing indifference into her expression. 'That will be all, thank you, Fredericks,' she said, turning to the butler. 'Dizzy, how nice to see you again!' Her words were the insincerely polite ones of a host having an unwanted guest foisted upon them, although her eyes were dancing with mischief as she looked at Dizzy.

Easily one of the most beautiful women Dizzy had ever seen, with glorious ebony hair and huge blue eyes, and a model-girl figure, Christi wasn't in the least conceited about her looks, but felt them merely to be her stock-in-trade for the career she had chosen for herself. She had even been warned that being too beautiful could hinder her career, rather than help it, if she was serious about becoming an actress of any repute.

The two women stood grinning at each other once they were alone in the high-ceilinged entrance hall, their breathing echoing hollowly against the grey stone.

'I thought you weren't coming.' Christi finally sighed her relief that she had been proved wrong.

Dizzy's smile widened. 'I needed a little time to wake up,' she teased, reminding her friend of the earliness of her call. 'Besides, how could I let down the person who probably stopped me being put in jail—at least overnight?' she mocked, thinking of her friend's efforts of bribery and corruption.

Christi looked embarrassed. 'I only——'

'What's going on here?'

Dizzy didn't need the confirmation of her friend's suddenly guiltily apprehensive expression to guess that the man who had silently entered the hall through another door was fusty, dusty Zachariah Bennett. He spoke quietly, but nevertheless with a complete assurance that he was entitled to the explanation he demanded. If he had come in on the conversation soon enough to overhear her reference to almost being put in jail, then that wasn't so surprising!

'Uncle Zach.' Christi quickly regained control, crossing to the man as he stood slightly in the shadows beneath the stairway, the door he had used just behind him, probably belonging to the kitchen or cellar, Dizzy thought. 'I asked you if an old school acquaintance of mine could come to stay,' Christi reminded lightly.

Dizzy turned to look at her; she had *told* her uncle of her visit? What had happened to the 'old acquaintance' who had just happened to be 'drifting' through, had 'heard Christi was in the area and decided to pay her a call'?

Christi had changed the story without warning her! But she wasn't able to dwell on that, as Zachariah Bennett at last stepped out of the shadows.

Baggy, and definitely *untailored* corduroys, a cream shirt that looked more than a little creased beneath the too-large tweed jacket, were exactly the sort of attire she had expected the bookishly austere Professor Zachariah Bennett to wear. But, as her wincing gaze rose, and she saw the gold-streaked blond hair, she knew that the ill-fitting clothing covered the magnificent body of the Greek god she had watched as he had swum naked not half an hour ago!

CHAPTER TWO

COULD this man have a twin brother, a man who looked exactly as he did, but who was the type to go skinny-dipping? That could be the only possible explanation for Zachariah Bennett having the same curiously light brown hair beneath gold that her Greek god had possessed. But Christi had told her numerous times that her uncle Zachariah was her only living relative, so that couldn't be the answer to the similarity. And Dizzy refused to believe there was another man in the area with the same beautiful-coloured hair. Which only left the one possibility she had started with: Zachariah Bennett was her naked Greek god.

Who would have believed that such a magnificent body lay beneath those hopelessly shapeless clothes? Obviously not Christi, or she wouldn't have called her uncle 'fusty and dusty'. Or maybe she would. Somehow, Christi had given her the impression that her uncle was an elderly man, but the mid-thirties this man must be wasn't that, either. At least, it didn't seem so to Dizzy. Maybe, to Christi, he just seemed old because he was her uncle. Whatever the reason, Dizzy knew that no man with a body like this one had, powerfully muscled and so blatantly male, could ever be fusty or dusty!

To give Christi her due, she had never seen him like that, and the rest of his appearance—his

clothed appearance, that was—didn't hint at anything other than the impression of a professor of
history. Oh, his face was handsome enough, even
if it was set in austere lines right now, his jaw square
and determined, with a barest hint of a cleft in the
chin, his mouth a tautly drawn line, although his
lips looked as if they might be sensual if he ever
relaxed them enough to let them be—and Dizzy
knew from her view of him earlier that he could be
very relaxed when he chose to be!

Black-rimmed glasses covered his eyes, but, even
so, she could see they were a beautiful light brown,
looking like golden warm honey. The lovely sun-
streaked hair, that had been drying in attractive
curls on his forehead earlier, was now brushed
severely to the side and back. He only needed a
pipe to complete the picture of the professor of history that he was!

Even as the amused thought crossed her mind,
she saw that his right hand was patting absently at
the bulging pocket of his tweed jacket, lean fingers
pulling out a well-used pipe that he clasped between strong white teeth as he began a vague hunt
for his matches.

The only thing wrong with the image was that
Dizzy couldn't get the memory of the naked Greek
god out of her mind!

Try as she might—and she had to admit she
wasn't trying *too* hard—she couldn't forget the ab-
solute vision of him as he stood in the sunlight,
letting the warmth of the day dry him off after his
swim. If she looked closely at him now she could
even see a couple of damp tendrils of hair behind
his ears, where the sun hadn't touched him. And

she knew she would never be able to feel in awe of him the way Christi obviously was; she could feel *aware* of him, yes, but never in awe of him!

But right now she had to try and fill in the gaps to Christi's new story about her visit. Obviously she was no longer 'drifting through', but what was she doing here? Nothing to recommend her, if what Christi was saying was to be believed!

'Poor dear,' she was telling her uncle. 'When Dizzy told me she had nowhere else to go...' She shook her head sadly.

Dizzy winced at the obvious implication; surely Christi was laying it on a bit thick, even if it was to show 'Uncle Zach' how kind and *responsible* she was!

She felt Zachariah Bennett's disapproving gaze on her, inwardly cringing at the role she was having to play in the name of friendship. In any other circumstances, she would have enjoyed meeting this man, would have been full of questions. Playing what was now turning out to be little better than a parasite didn't sit well with her.

She gave Zachariah Bennett a bright, meaningless smile, not able to meet his penetrating gaze, which was probably convincing him she was shiftless, too! 'Christi can be so kind,' she said noncommittally, still floundering in the dark a little.

Eyes, that should have been as warm to look at as the honey they resembled, frosted over as Zachariah Bennett's gaze raked over her with disgust. 'Kindness is not always the wisest thing,' he bit out coldly. 'In fact, in some circumstances, it is better to be cruel.'

'Oh no, Uncle Zach,' Christi protested with wide-eyed innocence. 'I told you, I couldn't bear to think of Dizzy having to—well, perhaps sleep on a park bench somewhere.' She sounded distraught at the idea.

As well she might do! What amazed Dizzy was that the possibility had even been mentioned between Christi and her uncle. *She* had been doing Christi the favour by pet-sitting her flat in the first place; there were plenty of other places she could have been. She had thought then that she was helping out a friend, but from the contemptuous look on the professor's face he believed every sad word of woe which Christi was feeding him!

'I'm sure I would have been able to find—somewhere else to go, if you hadn't been able to take me in,' she grated, giving Christi a warning look. Her friend was going a little too far, she felt!

'I'm sure you would,' Zachariah Bennett acknowledged distantly. 'But my niece considers she should help out an old school acquaintance when she can.'

Christi was visibly preening at the praise, and Dizzy just wanted to shake her. Not only was she a drifter and a wastrel, she *was* supposed to be a parasite, too!

As soon as she got Christi on her own she was going to tell her exactly what she thought of this new plan of hers. She might have 'cultivated' her life-style, but she had never taken advantage of anyone's kindness. And she had to admit she didn't like Zachariah Bennett thinking that she had; even the dark-rimmed glasses didn't hide the contempt for her in his eyes. Usually she didn't give a damn what people thought of her, or the way she lived, but with this man she did. And she wasn't about to analyse *that* too deeply.

'And as, for the moment, this is my niece's home,' he continued, 'may I also extend an invitation for you to stay with us,' he added grudgingly. 'Now if you'll excuse me, Christi, Miss——'

'James,' she supplied, realising, as he hesitated, that Christi hadn't told him *everything* about her. Her expression was bland as she sensed her friend's sharp gaze upon her. 'Dizzy James,' she enlarged.

'Miss James,' he nodded dismissively, puffing distractedly on the pipe, now that he had finally managed to get it lit. 'I'll leave you two to get re-acquainted, while I go and change.' He nodded, as if satisfied with his decision.

'Uncle Zach has been out bird-watching,' Christi explained indulgently.

Something suddenly seemed to be stuck in Dizzy's throat. She coughed chokingly, tears streamed down her cheeks, for the air couldn't reach her lungs. *Bird-watching?* Any birds that had been in Zachariah Bennett's vicinity half an hour ago had been watching *him*, curious of the unusual antics of the human in their midst!

'It's all right. I'm all right,' she gasped when she could finally find the strength to speak, firmly discouraging Christi from administering any more of the hearty slaps to the back she had been giving her since she first began to choke. 'Really, Christi, I'm fine.' She held up her hands defensively as her friend still looked undecided about administering one more slap for luck.

'The mention of ornithology seemed to have a strange effect on you?' Zachariah Bennett raised dark blond brows questioningly, once Dizzy was calm.

She kept her expression deliberately bland as she looked up at him. 'Not at all, Professor Bennett. In fact, the reason I was slightly later in arriving than I had said I would be was because I became interested in watching a bird myself.' A golden eagle, she decided.

The honey-brown gaze sharpened. 'Really?' he prompted harshly.

Still he didn't invite her to use the familiarity of his first name but, as he now seemed to think she had only said she had been bird-watching as a means of insinuating herself into his good graces, perhaps that was understandable! The sooner she and Christi had a private word the better.

'Oh yes,' she nodded. 'Christi will tell you, I'm very much into bird-watching.'

Christi gave her a glaring look. 'I really don't know your likes and dislikes that well, Dizzy,' she said through gritted teeth. 'It must be—how many years, since we last met?'

Dizzy gave her friend a reproachful frown. For all his absently distracted ways, she knew the professor to be a very intelligent man, and she and Christi were going to need to be very much on their guard to keep up the pretence Christi was getting them into more and more by the minute.

'I really can't remember,' she muttered warningly. 'But I'm sure it can't be that long ago.'

Christi gave an affected laugh. 'Dizzy seems to have moved around so much since we left school that she's forgotten time altogether,' she confided lightly to her uncle. 'Come on, Dizzy.' Her smile lacked warmth as she turned to her, her expression purposeful. 'I'll show you up to the room you're to use during your stay.'

Her friend's grip on her arm was only just short of vicelike, and Dizzy winced slightly, while trying to give the professor a reassuring smile. 'I do appreciate your kind invitation.'

He gave her a look which clearly indicated that if it had been left to him she would have been looking for the park bench, nodding curtly before moving agilely up the wide stone stairway.

Dizzy instantly turned to Christi as she pulled her towards the stairs. 'What do you——'

'Ssh,' her friend warned, looking frantically about them to see if they could be overheard. 'We can talk when we get to your room,' she muttered.

'But——'

'Dizzy, I am not in the mood to be argued with!' Her voice rose shrilly.

She did sound more than a little strained—and she was probably going to be even more so once Dizzy told her she didn't think this plan of hers could possibly work.

If only she could have spoken to Christi when she'd called earlier, or at least before she'd had to meet the uncle! The way things stood at the moment, she had no choice but to continue with the plan Christi had started before she'd arrived. Unfortunately, it was a plan she felt was doomed to failure, although Christi didn't agree with her.

They had strolled up the stairway together, Dizzy having assured Fredericks, when he quietly appeared back in the entrance hall, that she could manage her own shoulder-bag and backpack. She smiled, as if she hadn't seen his scandalised look that that was *all* of her luggage.

Christi gave her a running commentary as they went. 'Only the east wing has been renovated for habitation so far,' she pointed out, then explained why the rest of the castle was closed off to them. 'Uncle Zach has the work done as he gets the money. He must get paid very well to have the work done at all,' she added in a whispered aside. 'But what he's had done so far is lovely,' she continued in her normal voice.

For her uncle's benefit, Dizzy acknowledged wryly. There wasn't an angle possible that Christi wasn't playing, and it was all so unnecessary, when just being herself would probably have made the best impression.

The renovation that had so far been done to the castle was very impressive, and looked very much as it must have when it was first built in the fifteenth century. Dizzy realised it also had some of the discomfort that must have gone with it at that time, as she gave an involuntary shiver from the cold. Obviously Zachariah Bennett had gone for complete authenticity, omitting the central heating that might have made the castle more appealing. She could only hope that authenticity hadn't gone as far as the plumbing; carrying buckets of water up the stairs for her bath didn't exactly appeal to her!

'I've given you the bedroom next to mine.' Christi threw open the heavy oak door.

Dizzy was mesmerised from the first, from the tapestry that was the height and breadth of one wall, to the four-poster bed that totally dominated the huge room.

As she walked dazedly into the room, she touched the brocade curtains on the bed wonderingly, knowing by their thickness that they would pull completely around the sides and bottom of the bed, affording its occupant complete privacy. Her eyes aglow with pleasure, she walked across the room to gaze out of one of the long, narrow windows that graced two walls of the room. The view was magnificent—lakes and mountains as far as the eye could see. Heat warmed her cheeks as she realised that the small lake Zachariah Bennett had swum in earlier was just behind the first hill to the east, that it might even be part of the land that obviously adjoined the castle.

She was never going to get tired of the scenery if every time she looked out of this window she remembered Zachariah Bennett's nakedness so vividly!

'—so far, don't you think?'

She turned back to Christi, realising she had missed half the conversation in her musing over Zachariah Bennett. From the sudden impatience in Christi's expression, *she* had realised it, too!

'I said,' her friend bit out with slow emphasis, 'I think everything is going well so far, don't you? Or, at least, it would be, if you would enter into the spirit of the thing a bit more,' she added critically.

'Christi, I don't think this is going to work.' Dizzy put all thoughts of Zachariah Bennett's nakedness from her mind, as she concentrated on convincing Christi that her plan wasn't such a good one, after all.

Thankfully, she noted, as she turned back into the room, that an adjoining door revealed a fully fitted bathroom. It wouldn't be as good as a naked swim in a lake, but a bath would certainly refresh her!

'It's obvious you're trying to convince your uncle I'm some sort of leech,' she sighed. 'But, personally, I think you've gone over the top. You're making me out to be little more than a parasite to everyone I've ever known. No wonder he disliked me on sight!' she grimaced.

'Oh, that didn't have anything to do with being a leech,' Christi shook her head with certainty.

Her expression became wary. 'Then what did it have to do with?'

Christi shrugged. 'Henry.'

'Henry?' she repeated in a puzzled voice. 'What does your dog have to do with this?'

'Nothing, really.' Christi began to smile, starting to relax, at last.

'Then—Christi, what is going on?' she demanded impatiently.

Her friend was really having trouble not openly laughing now. 'Oh, Dizzy, it couldn't have worked out better if I'd planned it that way!' she said excitedly. 'Of course I didn't,' she assured hastily.

'What are you talking about?' she prompted warily, sure that, whatever 'it' was, it didn't augur well for her!

Christi grimaced. 'You remember this morning that I told you I heard someone coming, and quickly ended our call?'

'Vaguely,' she dismissed with a sigh. 'I don't function too well at six o'clock in the morning!'

'Well, apparently my uncle does,' Christi said drily. 'He was the one I heard. It seems he likes to take long walks first thing in the morning, before starting work for the day. He asked who I was talking to on the telephone.' She pulled a face. 'And so I explained that you had got my number from *another* schoolfriend, and asked if you could come and stay.'

That part of things seemed to be clear enough; it certainly explained the change of plans about her supposed arrival at the castle. 'OK, I accept that you had no choice about that,' she said wearily. 'Although I think you might have warned me about it,' she added sternly.

'I haven't had a minute to myself since I called you at six o'clock!' Christi protested indignantly. 'Uncle Zach insisted I join him for his walk, and then, when we got back, he watched over me while I ate a nauseously enormous breakfast.' She shuddered at the memory and Dizzy remembered that she was ordinarily only a coffee drinker for her first meal of the day. 'He thinks I don't eat enough,' she grimaced. 'Then, of all things, he decided we hadn't spent enough time together during my stay, and dragged me off for a tour of the area. I have never been so bored in my entire life, Dizzy. He really——'

'Christi, this is all very interesting,' she cut in with a decided lack of sympathy. 'But we seem to have forgotten Henry,' she reminded.

'Henry?' Her friend frowned. 'What on earth—oh! Oh, yes.' Her expression cleared, and she bit her lip to once again stop herself from smiling. 'Uncle Zach was quite shocked at the idea of your taking a man into your bed just because he has soulful brown eyes and looks lonely!'

'*Taking a man*——' Dizzy stared at her in horrified disbelief. '*What* man?' She shook her head dazedly.

Christi was choking with laughter. 'Surely you remember what you said on the telephone about——'

'—about letting *your dog* sleep at the foot of my bed,' she finished explosively, as she *did* remember. 'Are you telling me your uncle actually thinks Henry is a man?' Her eyes narrowed.

'Isn't it hilarious?' Her friend chuckled.

'Oh, hysterical,' she scorned. 'I may start screaming at any moment!' she groaned.

'Oh, come on, Dizzy,' Christi chided lightly. 'It's very funny.'

'Not if you're me. Or Henry,' she added disgustedly. 'We'll just have to hope his girlfriend down the road doesn't get to hear about this!'

'Hey,' Christi's eyes lit up with mischief as she ignored Dizzy's nonsensical ramblings, 'maybe what's really worrying my uncle is that *he* has brown eyes and must get very lonely here in this mausoleum!'

'His eyes aren't brown, they're golden,' Dizzy told her absently, colour warming her cheeks as she realised what she had said.

Luckily, Christi didn't seem to have taken any undue interest in the comment. It was testament to how disturbed by this situation her friend was that she hadn't noticed Dizzy's very personal observation about her uncle. Usually, Christi never ceased trying to interest her in one man or another, chagrined that Dizzy seemed able to keep her life man-free, while she somehow managed to attract a cluster of them, more often than not at the same time!

Dizzy could only breathe a sigh of relief at Christi's lack of attention just now, although she recognised it was mainly because her friend couldn't see that her uncle was an attractive man. But then, Christi *hadn't* seen him the way she had!

She gave an impatient sigh. 'Couldn't you have just explained to your uncle that Henry is your dog?'

'Of course not.' Christi sounded irritated. 'If I had done that, he would have realised you were pet-sitting at my flat. We aren't supposed to have seen each other for years,' she reminded. 'And *you* were supposed to have called me this morning!'

'Oh, I realise that.' She shook her head. 'You really went over the top with that "park bench" story,' she said disgustedly. 'Especially as I'm sure your uncle must have heard my comment about your having kept me out of spending a night in jail!'

'This isn't *all* my fault,' Christi returned caustically. '*You* were the one who told him your name is Dizzy James!'

'It *is* my name,' she said firmly. 'Professionally, at least. Besides, do you really think your uncle would have believed your story of my destitution if he had realised who my father is?' she drawled derisively.

'You're right.' Christi chewed worriedly on her bottom lip, then she grimaced. 'I told him your family lost all their money shortly after you left school. That was very quick thinking on your part, Dizzy,' she said thankfully.

Dizzy raised her eyes heavenwards. She hadn't given her name as James to try and further Christi's ridiculous plan, and Christi would have realised that if she was thinking in the least bit straight. Unfortunately, she wasn't. But Dizzy had given up using her father's name years ago, as she preferred not to be connected to him.

'I'm glad you approve,' she derided drily. 'Now, what are we going to do about this mess you've got us into by telling your uncle these outrageous lies?' She quirked blonde brows.

Christi looked wounded, and then a little sheepish, as Dizzy continued to meet her gaze mockingly. 'OK, so I'll have to think a little more before I speak,' she accepted uncomfortably. 'But other than that, everything is working out perfectly,' she defended. 'Since I told him about you, and the circumstances behind my inviting you to stay, my uncle hasn't mentioned the fact that I'm going to Drama School, and that I don't have the same boyfriend for more than a month at a time, sometimes less than that!'

'I'm glad to have been of service!' Dizzy's sarcasm was barely veiled.

Christi, however, seemed to have missed it completely in her feeling of self-satisfaction. 'I knew you would be.' She hugged her. 'Oh, Dizzy, it's so good to have you here!' she told her enthusiastically.

Her expression softened at her friend's genuine pleasure. 'It's good to be here,' she said wryly.

'It's going to be so much more fun now.' Christi smiled her delight.

Poor pet, thought Dizzy, she really looked as if she had been having a miserable time of it, although the vivacity was fast returning to her enormous blue eyes. 'I thought there was nothing to do,' she teased.

'There isn't,' Christi grimaced. 'But I can never remember a dull moment in your company in the past.' She brightened.

'I'm getting too old to be the class clown,' Dizzy dismissed absently, her gaze drawn towards the window that faced in the direction of the lake she had seen Zachariah Bennett in earlier. 'But, talking of things to do,' she turned interestedly back to Christi, 'does your uncle go—bird-watching, often?' She arched blonde brows expectantly.

'Most afternoons,' Christi confirmed in a bored voice. 'He says it helps relax him after a morning of intensely draining work!'

Skinny-dipping should certainly blow away the cobwebs!

'I don't honestly know why he bothers,' Christi added disgustedly. 'He only comes back and buries himself in work for another couple of hours!'

After his nude swim, he probably felt completely invigorated! 'It must be expensive maintaining a castle,' she pointed out softly.

'I suppose so,' Christi conceded grudgingly. 'But if he would just release my money I would be willing to help him out.'

Dizzy gave her friend a reproving look. 'I have a feeling your uncle takes his guardianship role very seriously, so for goodness' sake don't even think about offering him any money. I'm sure he would consider it a bribe.' And if his disapproving eyebrows rose any higher they would disappear into his hairline!

'I know that,' Christi dismissed impatiently. 'Or else I would have done it an hour after my arrival!' she added mischievously.

'I'm sure it can't be that bad here.' Dizzy shook her head ruefully, sure that a man like Zachariah Bennett would have an extensive library. Her fingers itched to touch all those wonderful books.

'Give it a few days,' Christi assured her. 'Even school was fun compared to this—and you know how I loved school!' she grimaced.

The daughter of a very happily married couple who unfortunately travelled a great deal, because Christi's father had been an archaeologist, Christi had been completely miserable at being sent away to boarding-school at only eight. It had been their mutual unhappiness with the situation they had both been thrust into that had initially drawn Dizzy and Christi together that first term. Over the years, they had become as close as sisters, helping each other through those difficult years. Dizzy had been able to keep Christi's spirits up, not because she didn't dislike the school as much as her friend did, but because, to her, it was preferable to being at home. Anything had been preferable to that!

'Look, I'll give you a few minutes' peace from my chattering while you shower and change—into something equally as disreputable, please!' she encouraged gleefully. 'And then I'll show you around—what there is to see!' She made a face.

Dizzy nodded, her smile fading once her friend had left, her attention once again drawn to that window that faced east.

Just over that small tree-covered hill lay the lake where Zachariah Bennett had bathed naked. And, if Christi was right about the 'bird-watching', he did the same thing every afternoon...

CHAPTER THREE

WHY hadn't she told Christi about seeing her uncle bathing nude?

The two of them had been together for a couple of hours before they parted to change for dinner, and yet she had remained silent about what she had seen at the lake. And she knew that knowing something like that would certainly help to relax Christi. How could Zachariah Bennett preach to Christi about irresponsibility when only hours ago he had been bathing in a spot where anyone could come along and witness it? She had since learnt that the lake area was part of the castle estate, but, even so, the act hardly fitted in with the professor's 'fusty, dusty' image.

And that was partly what kept her silent.

Christi was right when she claimed Dizzy had deliberately cultivated her life-style of having no tangible ties, where, quite literally, she carried all that she owned on her back. And that also meant, quite contrary to what Zachariah Bennett had been led to believe, that there had been no men in her life. Somehow, admitting to Christi what she had seen that afternoon wouldn't make that true any more. Christi would want to know all the intimate details, and most prominent in her memory of that afternoon was her own response and attraction to a man she had labelled a 'Greek god'—Christi's uncle, a man who believed she went to bed with a man for no better reason than he looked lonely and had soulful brown eyes!

She had spent years evading emotional entanglement, having a small circle of friends that she knew she could rely on completely, and who could rely on her, too. But, like Christi, most of those friends would have liked to see her happily in love, with perhaps a family of her own. Only her lightly dismissive attitude towards men had kept them from anyserious matchmaking on her behalf. And she felt far from lightly dismissive where Zachariah Bennett was concerned!

And so she hugged the memory of that afternoon to herself, wondering how long it would be before she gave in to the temptation to return to that lake one afternoon during her stay...

'Knollsley Hall in Cornwall,' remarked an abrupt voice from behind her.

Dizzy spun around as if she had been caught in the act of stealing the family silver, rather than merely gazing up at one of the paintings that adorned the stone walls in the room that had been made into quite a comfortable lounge.

Having showered shortly after she arrived, she had merely had a quick wash and changed her clothes when she had returned from the tour of the castle. Consequently Christi was still relaxing in the bath when she was ready to go down to dinner, and so she had come down without her, indulging in a more leisurely look around. Christi's whistle-stop— and obviously uninterested—tour had merely brushed the surface of it.

The first things to capture her attention in the lounge were the magnificent paintings on the walls, in particular, the one she now stood in front of, and which Zachariah Bennett had just supplied information about.

She had changed into one of the only two dresses she owned, the 'simple little black number' that was supposed to be suitable for any occasion, but which she dragged about with her merely because it didn't get creased in her backpack!

Unfortunately, Christi had been right about the 'freezer' temperatures in the castle, and so the sleeveless style of the dress wasn't 'suitable' at all! The only visible heating she had seen so far was the fire roaring away in the cavernous grate in this room, and for all its size it didn't even take the chill off the room. At least she had left her long hair loose tonight, so that her ears weren't actually freezing off! However, the wild tumble of blonde curls gave her the look of a wild wanton. No doubt Christi would be delighted with her appearance, although the professor looked far from pleased!

The black evening suit and white shirt were a definite improvement on his previous appearance. At least, they would have been, if the suit had been in the least tailored to the magnificence of his body, and the collar of his shirt wasn't sticking up on one side! The fact that his hair was newly washed, and once again brushed severely back from his face, didn't add to his attraction either, and his pipe seemed to have gone out long ago, although it was still clamped between his teeth to the side of his mouth.

To Dizzy, he just looked all the more endearing because of his lack of the sophisticated perfection that most of the men she had met in the past seemed to consider a must if they were to be successful with women. Maybe if she hadn't seen how beautiful he was beneath his ill-fitting clothing she might have accepted the face-value impression of the absent-minded professor, but her first sight of him had made that impossible.

'It's the house of the MP Martin Ellington-James,' he added, breaking her prolonged silence.

Her indulgent smile faded as she turned dutifully back to the painting of the gothic manor house, the artist having captured the cold ugliness of it perfectly. 'Quite impressive,' she said non-committally.

'Valerie Sherman is the artist,' he continued, as if even the polite conversation was a strain to him.

Dizzy turned back to him, transfixed, as she found his attention was riveted on the painting, those golden eyes aglow with admiration. Her breath caught in her throat at how breathtakingly handsome he was, and she couldn't help wondering what it must feel like if he looked at a woman in that way. She would like to see him without his glasses, and couldn't help wondering if he really needed to wear them when he wasn't working, or if they were some sort of shield to him. His eyesight had seemed perfectly all right this afternoon as he swam in the lake . . . Colour heated her cheeks as, once again, her thoughts unconsciously returned to that time.

'She used to live there, I believe.' He spoke tersely now.

Dizzy blinked, giving a self-conscious grimace as she realised Zachariah Bennett had stopped looking at the painting and was now looking at her—and was obviously wondering what she found so fascinating about him. She doubted he would look quite so impatiently polite if he knew the truth about that!

'I believe you're right,' she confirmed drily.

Honey-gold eyes widened. 'You know something about paintings and their artists?'

'Something,' she nodded wryly.

He couldn't completely keep the surprise out of his expression. 'You like Miss Sherman's paintings?' He seemed relieved to have found a subject he could talk to her about while they waited for Christi to join them.

'I appreciate good paintings,' she evaded, not really wanting to get into a discussion about this particular one. 'I don't think there can be any doubt that Valerie Sherman is a talented artist,' she added abruptly. 'She's certainly captured the sheer ugliness of Knollsley Hall perfectly!'

His attention returned to the painting. 'Perhaps it is a little——'

'Grotesque,' Dizzy supplied abruptly.

'Possibly,' he nodded. 'Although it's haunting, too.'

The reason Dizzy hated the painting of Knollsley Hall was because it was too lifelike!

'I have other Shermans,' the professor told her lightly. 'Ones that perhaps aren't so—gothic. You must let me show them to you some time.'

It was the politely meaningless offer of a host to a guest in his house—even an unwanted one—and Dizzy accepted it as such. He had no real desire to show her the Valerie Sherman paintings, and she certainly had no interest in seeing them.

'I'd like that.' She turned away from the disturbing painting. 'I—oh, excuse me,' she said awkwardly, as an involuntary shiver racked her body. 'I—it's a little chilly in here,' she excused with a grimace.

A ghost of a smile lightened his austere features. 'Not at all what you're used to, I'm sure.'

Oooh, ouch! Dizzy acknowledged ruefully. Obviously, he believed that when she sponged off her friends she made sure it was only the ones who could give her all the creature comforts!

Her gaze was widely innocent. 'It's certainly an improvement on a park bench.'

His mouth twisted as he stepped back from her. 'Come and stand beside the fire,' he ordered curtly. 'Would you really have slept on a park bench tonight?' he probed softly, as she obediently joined him beside the fire.

She sent up a few silent words of reproach to Christi for the lies she had entangled them in. A park bench, indeed! 'I'm really not sure,' she dismissed non-committally.

Gold eyes raked over her speculatively. 'I'm sure it's never actually come to that,' he said coldly. 'Probably—Henry would have been able to help out again.'

Dizzy drew in a sharp breath. Where was the instigator of all these lies when she needed her? 'I don't think so.' She shook her head. 'I—he's sleeping with someone else tonight.' Good lord, she was doing it herself now!

'I see,' Zachariah Bennett bit out abruptly. 'Do you see much of Christi when you're both in London?'

Nothing like finding out straight away whether or not she was a constant bad influence on his niece! 'I believe she told you that we haven't seen each other for years,' she dismissed. 'I can't tell you what a piece of luck it was to find out Christi was staying up here.' At least that was true; she wouldn't have got to meet him or see his castle if Christi hadn't been staying here, and she wouldn't have wanted to miss either one of them!

'Exactly why are you in the area, Miss James?'

'Dizzy, please,' she invited for a second time— while she frantically tried to think of a reason she *could* be in the Lake District. Her expression cleared as the most obvious one occurred to her. 'I—er— needed to get out of London for a while,' she told him lightly, keeping her expression deliberately bland.

He frowned. 'Henry—has a wife?' he rasped.

And she had always thought a professor of history couldn't have an imagination! 'No, nothing like that,' she dismissed without rancour. 'I just— well, I wanted to get away for a while. I'm sure you know how it is.' She gave him a bright smile.

'No—no, I can't say that I do. Could I get you a drink?' he offered abruptly, looking as if *he* certainly needed one.

If a drink would help thaw her out, then she would have half a dozen of them! Although, if she asked for the whisky that would have warmed her, she was sure Zachariah Bennett would be convinced she was an alcoholic on top of everything else he seemed to think she was!

'Just a small sherry, please,' she accepted with another shiver.

'Perhaps you should go and get yourself a cardigan,' he suggested as he saw the shiver. 'I don't feel the cold myself, but Christi assures me the evenings can be chill. I'm sure Christi would be glad to let you borrow something of hers if you don't have a sweater with you,' he added at her hesitation.

Well, really, he was going too far, even for the parasite he thought her to be. 'Thank you, I have one of my own—it comes in handy for the nights on the park bench,' she said sharply.

His gaze narrowed as he handed her the glass of sherry. 'Don't your parents worry about—the life you lead?'

'Not at all,' she answered truthfully; the lectures from her father had stopped long ago—about the same time he had lost interest in her completely! 'They have problems of their own,' she shrugged.

'Of course,' he accepted, still believing Christi's story of the financial difficulty of Dizzy's parents.

'The castle doesn't have any heating other than individual fires?' she asked, in the hope of changing the subject.

'Not yet,' he replied distantly, the frown between his eyes seeming to indicate that the question irritated him.

'It's a wonderful place,' she enthused, her earlier antagonism gone as her eyes glowed with interest. 'Do you——'

'Sorry I'm late.' Christi burst smilingly into the room. 'Here, Dizzy, I brought you this to wear, in case you didn't have one.' She held out a cream cashmere cardigan.

Dizzy gave her friend a frowning look as she absently took the garment and pulled it on, noting that Christi's face was a little flushed and she was breathing heavily—almost as if she had *been running*!

She gave Christi a hard glare as she realised that that was exactly what she had been doing, that her friend must have been standing outside the lounge door when she and Zachariah Bennett had the conversation about cardigans, that Christi must have rushed back up to her room to get her one, just to add to the impression of Dizzy's destitution. Only this afternoon she had cautioned Christi to ease up a bit, and here she was making it look as if even the clothes on her back were borrowed!

'Thank you,' she accepted in a hard tone, uncaring of the fact that the cashmere cardigan was making her feel a lot warmer.

She had been going to ask Zachariah Bennett about the history of the castle, but now the moment was lost, and she felt sure that Christi had spoilt it deliberately. Christi seemed determined to let her uncle believe their school had produced an idiot, rather than let him realise she had an avid interest in his own subject. Obviously she and Christi were going to have to have another little chat—and soon!

'You're very welcome,' Christi dismissed, putting her arm through the crook of her uncle's. 'Have the two of you been getting acquainted?' she prompted brightly.

How could she become genuinely acquainted with a man who believed the things about her that Zachariah Bennett did! And that was a great pity, because she found him very interesting indeed.

'Yes,' he answered Christi curtly. 'Could I get you a drink before dinner?'

'Just my usual juice,' she accepted lightly.

The only time Dizzy could remember Christi drinking juice was when they were at school, and then it had only been because it was that or milk, and she couldn't stand milk! Christi was going to go home from this visit with a halo if she didn't take care.

'Dizzy?'

She gave a start at Zachariah's first use of her name, finding she liked the slightly husky tone to his voice as he said it. 'I'm fine with my sherry, thanks.' She refused another drink. She knew it would have pleased Christi immensely if she had said yes, but as she usually drank very little she wasn't about to change *that* for Christi's benefit.

Ordinarily, she wouldn't have minded this situation, would have been glad just to help Christi out, knowing her friend really was mature enough to handle her own affairs. But she found she intensely disliked this false impression of her that she and Christi were so determined to give Zachariah Bennett. She would probably never see him again after this brief visit, never have to worry *what* he believed about her, but she couldn't help disliking it all, none the less.

'Cut it out, Christi,' she muttered, once the professor had crossed the huge, high-ceilinged room to get Christi's juice.

Her friend looked at her with innocently wide blue eyes. 'What do you mean?'

'The cardigan,' she sighed.

'Don't you like it?'

'I love it,' she muttered. 'What I didn't like was your perfectly timed interruption with it!'

Blue eyes flashed. 'Well, what do you mean by talking to him about his precious castle?' Christi attacked. 'That isn't going to help your image at all.'

'As you obviously heard *all* of our conversation,' she muttered sarcastically, keeping a wary eye on the broad back of Zachariah Bennett as he stood in front of the drinks' cabinet, 'you must have realised that my reputation has already taken enough of a beating tonight. It's time to give it a rest, Christi.' She sighed again. 'Unless you *want* your uncle to become so worried by my presence here that he tells you to ask me to leave?'

Christi looked panic-stricken. 'You really think I'm going too far?'

'About three hours ago,' she said drily. 'And you could have warned me about the Shermans.'

'I——'

'Tell me,' Zachariah Bennett looked at Dizzy as he turned back to them, crossing the room to hand Christi her juice, 'how did you come by the unlikely name of Dizzy?'

She glared at her friend as she almost choked over her juice. 'Unlikely, Professor Bennett?' she returned coolly. 'Most people consider it suits me very well.' She deliberately ignored the mischief glowing in Christi's eyes.

'Surely it isn't your given name?' he frowned.

'I didn't say that,' she shrugged. 'Although it's the only one I'll answer to!'

She cringed every time she thought of the names her father had let her mother give her. At the time, he had been so disappointed she wasn't the son he had wanted, that there could be no more children, that he hadn't cared what the daughter he hadn't wanted was named. It had only been later, when the shock had worn off, that he had realised how totally unsuitable his only child's names were. Out of desperation he had begun to call her by her initials of DC, but with the mischievous humour of children, those initials had become Dizzy once she began school.

To her mother she was still—but she was in total agreement with her father about *those* two names, it was probably the only thing the two of them *had* ever agreed upon! To her father she was still DC— when he called her anything, which he probably didn't do any more! But to everyone else she had been Dizzy since she was eight years old. And she intended remaining that way!

Zachariah Bennett gave the ghost of a smile. 'And I usually answer to Zach, or Zachariah, if you prefer. Only my students ever called me Professor!'

At last! It was a little unnerving to think of a man who affected her as deeply as this one did by the formal title of 'Professor', or the equally unsuitable 'Zachariah Bennett'. 'Zach, I think.' She smiled warmly. 'Thank you.'

He nodded curtly, as if he already regretted the impulse. 'I'm sure dinner should be ready by now.' He strode out of the room to find out why it obviously wasn't.

'That must be a first,' Christi murmured a little dazedly.

Dizzy frowned at her, her thoughts miles away from the coldness of this room—well, at least *two* miles away! 'What must?' she prompted with slight impatience.

'Didn't you notice?' Christi mused. 'He actually seemed—self-conscious, not at all like his usual arrogant self.'

Arrogant? The professor? She didn't believe it! 'I think you've just got used to a lack of parental influence, love,' she teased. 'Besides the fact that your uncle obviously disapproves of me—as you've meant him to do—he's been perfectly polite.'

'*I've* got used to a lack of parental influence?' Christi returned indignantly. 'What about you and your——'

'Let's leave my parents out of this, shall we?' cut in Dizzy warningly.

'Sorry.' Her friend looked shame-faced. 'I think you're right, the strain of all this is getting to me. But, you know,' she frowned, 'it gave me a whole new perspective of my uncle when he asked you to call him Zach,' she admitted ruefully.

Dizzy gave her an indulgent smile. 'What did you expect me to call him, "Uncle Zach"?'

Christi smiled, shaking her head. 'I've just never thought of him as just Zach before,' she shrugged.

'Hm,' she conceded wryly. 'But he must obviously be your father's younger brother?'

Christi nodded. 'By ten years. I know he looks—and *acts*—years older, but he's only thirty-five,' she grimaced.

Maybe as Professor Bennett he did look older than that, but as her 'Greek god' he looked much younger! And as time was passing Dizzy was having more and more difficulty separating the two.

'—would have that effect on you,' Christi was saying sadly.

'Sorry?' she prompted, sure from Christi's expression that she had missed something important.

Christi gave her a reproving look for her lack of attention. 'I said, I suppose a love affair that ended unhappily would have that effect on you,' she repeated patiently. 'Although it happened so long ago, I'm sure he has to be over it by now,' she frowned.

'It?' Dizzy asked with casual uninterest.

'My uncle's fiancée died—oh, almost eleven years ago now,' her friend explained thoughtfully. 'It was such a shame, she was so nice. I remember she used to make clothes for my favourite doll of the time,' she murmured fondly.

'Mercenary little baggage, aren't you?' Dizzy teased drily, all the time her thoughts on Zachariah Bennett's tragic loss. Eleven years ago, and from what Christi had said there hadn't been another serious relationship since; he must have loved his fiancée very much. It just confirmed her belief that loving people hurt too much, took too much, while seeming to give nothing back.

'I didn't mean she was nice because of that,' Christi retorted indignantly, relaxing with a rueful smile as she saw Dizzy's teasing expression. 'I only used the example of the doll's clothes to show you how nice she was, how she even had time for the objectionable brat I was at the time... Some people might say I haven't changed all that much,' she added ruefully, as Dizzy looked even more amused.

'Really?' Dizzy returned innocently.

Christi grinned. 'I can't imagine how you've been able to stand me the last twelve years!'

'It hasn't been easy.' She gave a heavily affected sigh.

'But you've muddled through,' Christi derided.

'Someone had to take pity on you and be your friend.' Dizzy sounded as if she had the weight of responsibility on her shoulders.

Christi grimaced at her sacrificial expression. 'There hasn't been a day gone by during those years when I haven't been grateful that you were the one to do that,' she told her seriously. 'Sometimes I don't know what I would have done without you.'

Dizzy squeezed her shoulder, knowing the death of Christi's parents three years ago had been a terrible shock to her, that without the support and love of her friends at that time Christi might have broken down completely. Christi had gone to stay with her uncle for a few weeks after the accident, but the real shock hadn't seemed to set in until she had been back in London for several weeks. And then it had been up to her friends to rally round, Dizzy most of all, to make sure that she didn't fall apart. If anything, the tragedy had brought the two girls even closer together, Dizzy having looked up to Christi's parents more than she did her own.

'It was mutual,' Dizzy said huskily, thinking of all the times Christi had helped her when she had been upset or alone. 'Although,' she added briskly, 'I think you might have made some effort to warn me about the Shermans your uncle seems so proud of.' She looked reproving.

Christi blushed, grimacing. 'I was hoping you wouldn't notice them,' she said apologetically.

Dizzy gave her a chiding look. 'Not notice *that* monstrosity?' She nodded at the huge painting of Knollsley Hall across the room.

'It's awful, isn't it?' Christi winced. 'He has several others, too,' she admitted reluctantly.

'So he told me,' she acknowledged drily. 'Although I doubt any of them could be as ghastly as that one!'

'Well, actually...'

'Dinner is finally ready.' An impatient Zachariah Bennett returned to the lounge, effectively cutting off what Christi had been about to say. 'It appears there was some sort of panic in the kitchen,' he apologised abruptly.

'Anything serious?' Christi prompted concernedly.

'Fredericks assures me everything is under control now,' her uncle dismissed.

Obviously he was a man who didn't like his routine upset, and that included any delay in the serving of meals, Dizzy thought with some amusement, as they went through to the dining-room for their meal.

Everything new she learnt about this man made him all the more endearing to her. And it wasn't an emotion she particularly welcomed.

Possibly, at the moment, she should be more concerned with Christi's unfinished comment of, 'Well, actually...' concerning the Sherman paintings...

CHAPTER FOUR

'WHAT on earth are you doing?'

Dizzy froze, wincing as she slowly withdrew from within the huge larder she had been searching through so avidly seconds earlier.

She ran her hands nervously down her thighs as she reluctantly turned to face Zachariah Bennett. Talk about being caught in the act! Here she was, raiding the larder, and she had been caught at it by none other than her host.

The first thing she noticed, as she looked across the brightly lit kitchen at him, was that he bought his pyjamas from the same chain-store she did, for their blue and white striped pyjamas were matching pairs!

She laughed, she just couldn't help it. 'Snap!' she managed to murmur before laughing again.

Zach wore a blue woollen robe over his pyjamas, neatly tied at his waist, although the rest of his appearance wasn't quite as neat: his hair falling across his forehead in soft curls, his glasses missing altogether. Obviously he had left his bedroom in rather a hurry.

Probably hoping to catch a burglar, Dizzy acknowledged ruefully, sobering as she realised he didn't look too pleased about having had his sleep interrupted.

'I was—er—I fancied a midnight snack.' She lamely explained her presence in the kitchen.

He glanced at the clock on the wall. 'It's one-thirty in the morning,' he said drily.

Without his glasses, the full impact of those honey-coloured eyes was inescapable; Dizzy was completely lost in their depths at first glance.

'Dizzy?' He frowned at her lack of response to his comment.

She blinked, momentarily breaking the spell. 'I—I fancied a one-thirty-in-the-morning snack,' she said, giving a rueful shrug.

'Didn't you have enough to eat at dinner time?' He arched blond brows.

'Oh, yes,' she nodded. 'I just—I always get hungry this time of night,' she grimaced.

'I see,' he sighed, relaxing slightly. 'Well, what were you looking for? Perhaps I could help you,' he offered, in the way of a man who just wanted to get this over with so that he could go back to bed.

It wasn't very complimentary to her, Dizzy acknowledged ruefully. OK, so the striped pyjamas weren't the sexiest nightwear in the world, but they were *all* she was wearing; there should have at least been a spark of sexual awareness in those golden eyes. Instead, Zach was looking at her much the same as the teachers had at boarding-school when they caught the boarders having a tuck-party in their dormitory after lights-out!

'Pilchards,' she sighed, for the first time wishing to see those instant thoughts of bed that came into a man's eyes when they looked at her—and not with sleep in mind, either! She had been plagued by her 'bedroom' body all her adult life, and now, when she somehow *wanted* Zach to notice her, he couldn't see past the schoolgirl acquaintance of his niece!

His eyes widened. 'I beg your pardon?'

She smiled at his complete lack of comprehension. 'It's a fish,' she provided lightly. 'Belonging to the herring family. A bit like a large sardine,' she added as he still looked unimpressed. 'They come in tins, in either tomato sauce or oil,' she explained further.

He still didn't look impressed. 'Really?'

'Yes,' she nodded frantically.

Zach crossed his arms across his chest. 'And you expected to find some of them in my larder?' he prompted patiently.

'I—well—I thought everyone had pilchards in their kitchen store-cupboard,' she said lamely, guessing by his deadpan expression that the fish had never had a place in *his* store-cupboard! 'Maybe some sardines, then,' she suggested hopefully.

She wasn't sure if it was her imagination, or if she really did see a glimmer of amusement in the golden depths. And then it had disappeared completely, his expression even more fierce than before.

'You aren't pregnant, are you?' came the instant explanation for that fierceness.

Much as she loved Henry, and hated to see that soulful expression in his big brown eyes, she wished now that she had never let the little devil go to sleep on the bottom of her bed!

'No,' she answered irritably. 'I just happen to like pilchards.'

'Well, you won't find any in here,' Zach bit out. 'Why don't you try the fridge? There might be a drumstick or two in there.'

'Anything else but pilchards keeps me awake if I eat it this time of night.' She shook her head.

He looked as if just the *thought* of eating the revolting-sounding fish might keep him awake for the rest of the night! 'I'm afraid I can't help you.' He stepped pointedly away from the doorway.

Dizzy hung back, knowing she wasn't going to be able to sleep just yet. When she had finally managed to speak to Christi on her own she had been most disturbed by what her friend had to tell her. After reading for three hours—they had all gone to bed at ten-thirty—having finished the Claudia Laurence book she had been enjoying so much, she still hadn't felt tired enough to fall asleep as she usually did after a long read. Sitting down with a tin of pilchards and a mug of hot milk usually worked if all else failed.

'Could I—is it all right if I have some hot milk instead?' She looked at Zach hopefully.

'Of course,' he agreed with barely concealed impatience. 'Would you like me to get it for you?'

'No, I—sorry.' She gave an awkward grimace as an involuntary shiver racked her body. 'The kitchen seems to have cooled down since dinner was cooked in here.' She hastily set about pouring the milk into a saucepan to put on to heat.

'Here.'

She turned abruptly as she felt the warmth of the woollen garment about her shoulders, blinking dark lashes over wide green eyes as she realised that the suddenness of her movement had put her and Zach into a closeness that meant their pyjama-clad bodies were only inches apart.

Zach looked taken aback by the sudden tension of the situation, and stared down at her intently, neither of them seeming capable of movement.

Dizzy had never felt so aware of a man. The V of his pyjama jacket revealed the start of the golden hair she knew covered the whole of his chest, and lower. That chest moved up and down rapidly, and she knew in that moment that he was just as aware of her as she was him, that the fusty, dusty façade of Professor Bennett had a wide crack in it.

Quite what would have happened next Dizzy didn't like to guess, although she hoped, for the sake of her peace of mind, that they would have moved apart as they were doing now, she to snatch the saucepan of milk from the top of the cooker as it began to boil over, Zach to stand across the room from her.

Her hand shook slightly as she poured the hot milk into a mug, the robe about her shoulders slipping to the floor as she reached out to put water in the used saucepan. She tensed as she heard the pad of Zach's slipper-clad feet on the tiled floor; still facing the sink, she felt his presence behind her.

'Turn around,' he instructed gruffly.

She drew in a ragged breath as she reluctantly did as he asked, finding him standing in front of her, holding out the robe for her to put her arms into.

'You need it more than I do,' he prompted as she hesitated. 'There isn't too much of you to keep you warm,' he added derisively, as she slipped her arms into the too-big robe.

Obviously he considered her nomadic life-style didn't provide enough food for her to get fat. He probably thought she had been raiding his larder for the same reason! After an evening of feeling as if he must consider her a charity case, she wasn't in the mood for further reminding of the role she was supposed to be playing!

'I'm not small all over,' she pointed out with deliberate provocation.

Zach faltered only slightly in the act of turning up the too-long sleeves, looking up into her face reprovingly, although Dizzy noticed his gaze didn't return immediately to the sleeve he was working on after leaving her face, but lingered on the suddenly uneven rise and fall of her breasts.

'There.' He stepped back with some relief once he had completed the task. 'You look like a child trying to appear older by dressing up in an adult's clothes,' he murmured, this time the amusement in his eyes completely obvious.

Her eyes flashed at the condescension of unmistakable maturity. 'Does anything you've heard about me lead you to believe I'm still a child, in any way?' she challenged.

He stiffened, his expression suddenly harsh.

'Oh, look, I'm sorry.' Dizzy gave a weary sigh. 'It's been a long day, and I'm feeling a little disgruntled because I can't seem to get to sleep.'

'Possibly it's the unusual occurrence of sleeping alone that's causing the disturbance,' he told her frostily.

If he didn't so obviously mean every word he was saying, it might have been funny: she was the original virgin, hadn't even been kissed properly in her twenty-one years. Although she had a feeling she might have come close to it a few minutes ago!

It was because she knew how close she had come to being bent to the will of another person that her reply was made so caustically. 'You're probably right,' she snapped. 'Perhaps you would like to offer to rectify that?' Her chin rose challengingly.

His mouth twisted. 'I don't believe so, thank you,' he said with obvious distaste.

'Why not?' she taunted. 'Aren't I good enough for you?'

'I'm sure you're very good,' he drawled contemptuously. 'Fortunately,' he stressed the word, 'I'm not attracted to over-experienced children! Your milk is cooling,' he added coldly. 'I'm sure I can leave you alone to enjoy it.'

'Aren't you frightened I might steal the family silver, a painting or two, and just sneak off into the night?' she mocked hardly.

He drew in an angry breath. 'No.'

'Why not?' she derided.

He shrugged. 'The silver—what there is of it— is locked away, and the paintings are all wired to an alarm.'

Dizzy's mouth twisted. 'I might have known it wasn't a question of trusting me!'

Zach gave a weary sigh. 'How long have you had that chip on your shoulder?'

'I think I was probably born with it,' she said ruefully, knowing that she did have a defensive shield that usually kept the world out. Except that this man had been able to get under her guard. One moment she didn't mind that he had, even welcomed it, and the next moment she wanted her shield back in place again. She wasn't used to these feelings of insecurity, not any more.

He shook his head. 'I'm sure there's a wealth of conversation to be made from that comment, unfortunately it's too late—or early, depending on your point of view,' he said drily, 'to go into right now. Don't forget to turn the lights off before you go back to bed,' he advised briskly.

'Your robe.' Dizzy stopped him at the door.

'You can return it tomorrow,' he dismissed abruptly. 'Maybe you would also like to go into town and get in a store of—pilchards——' he named the fish as if he even found saying them difficult! '—as you seem to be addicted to them,' he added derisively.

She looked at him with innocently wide eyes. 'What will I do for money?'

He sighed, as if he had half been expecting that question. 'I have an account at one of the stores in town. Just tell them it's for the Castle Haven, and it will be OK.'

'You're so kind,' she mocked softly.

'As I told you earlier today,' he rasped coldly. 'It can sometimes be kinder to be cruel.'

Dizzy sat down shakily once he had abruptly left the room, knowing that this round had definitely gone to Zach. She had allowed temper and resentment to overrule good sense, her defences going into overdrive as she realised how close she had come to allowing an emotion other than friendship into her life. But at least she had managed to so disgust Zach that the closeness wasn't likely to happen again.

Zach was a man who had lost, to death, the woman he loved; he certainly didn't need the complication of someone like her in his life. And she, well, she made a point of keeping *all* complications out of her life!

Dizzy was up early the next morning, for the main reason that she hadn't been to sleep.

The milk had done little but fill her up so that she felt uncomfortable. So, instead of going to sleep as she had planned, she had dug to the bottom of her bag and pulled out yet another of her favourite books, and read her way through that until seven o'clock, mindful of the fact that Christi said her uncle usually left the castle at six-thirty to go for his morning walk.

Christi was still fast asleep when she glanced in on her, lying serenely back on the pillows, not a hair out of place. Even in sleep Christi was beautiful, Dizzy acknowledged ruefully.

Her own appearance wasn't quite as neat, her hair once again plaited down her spine, the usual wisps escaping about her face and neck. She wore a different T-shirt from yesterday, although it was just as baggy, and the same patched jeans from the day before. She had noted with rueful acceptance that there were even several freckles across her nose today from her walk in the sunshine yesterday. If Zach *had* found her childlike the night before, it wasn't so surprising!

She was looking for the library, knowing that it was there she would find what she sought. Christi had told her last night that it was there, and the sooner she got the confrontation over, the better it would be. Much better that she should do it alone, too. Maybe, then, she might even be able to start sleeping again.

Her hands were clammy, her heart beating wildly, as she looked for the book-lined room, even the thought of the books not able to detract from that other ugliness.

As she passed the corridor leading to the kitchen, she thought she heard a child crying, and felt a shiver down her spine, her memories so vividly disturbing that she knew that haunting unhappiness was once again with her, making her imagine things, that the child she could hear crying was herself, the child deep inside her which had had to die so that she might live.

But as she heard the cry again she realised it was a real cry, that there was a child in the kitchen, crying as if its heart would break!

She couldn't bear the pain behind that cry, and she hurried down the corridor to throw open the kitchen door.

Seated at the table, her arms about a little girl of perhaps four or five, was the cook, her stricken face evidence that she was greatly disturbed by the interruption.

Dizzy was too concerned by the little girl's distress to worry about the middle-aged woman's feelings. Going down on her haunches, she smiled gently into the most angelically beautiful face she had ever seen, dark hair framing that little face, deep blue eyes tear-wet, a tiny snub nose, and a tiny quivering mouth.

'Hello,' Dizzy said warmly. 'I'm very hungry for my breakfast, aren't you?' She sat down in the chair on the other side of the little girl, taking over the task of feeding her the toast the cook was having so much trouble with. 'Could I have some of this lovely toast too, please?' she requested of the cook, as the wide-eyed little girl took a bite of the toast she held out to her temptingly. Realising that the dumb-struck obedience wouldn't last once the little girl got over her shyness, she knew she had to distract her attention. 'My name's Dizzy, what's yours?' She held the little girl's gaze as the cook slowly got to her feet to prepare more toast.

'Dizzy?' the little girl echoed sceptically, revealing that she had a slight lisp from where her two front teeth were missing.

'That's right,' Dizzy grinned. 'And I bet your name is something pretty, like Annabel, or Melissa, or——'

'I want Melissa,' the little girl cried, her lips quivering again as tears flooded and overflowed her eyes. 'I want Melissa!' she sobbed in earnest.

Dizzy put down the toast, turning enquiringly to the distressed cook at the emotional outburst she had provoked.

'She woke up in the night asking for her,' the other woman said frantically. 'Her mother—that's my daughter, was rushed into hospital yesterday, and Kate's been with me ever since. Her father's away on business, although he's going to be back tomorrow. I've tried to explain to Kate that she'll be able to see all her friends again soon, but she still keeps asking for this Melissa.' She sounded completely frayed.

'Kate.' Dizzy turned back to the little girl as she buried her fists in her eyes, still sobbing noisily.

'Your Mummy isn't well just now, and so Nanny is taking care of you,' she explained gently. 'Nanny is very upset you can't be with your friends just now, but——'

'I want Melissa!' the little girl wailed.

Dizzy felt the constriction of her heart at the pained plea, watching impotently as the little girl jumped up and ran from the room.

'I just don't know what to do.' The cook sat down wearily in the chair opposite Dizzy's, looking completely frazzled. 'Maureen—Kate's mother, was rushed to hospital with appendicitis. It was all such a panic, but once we knew the operation had been a success I brought Kate back here with me.' She sighed. 'There are some children in the house next door to Kate's, maybe this Melissa is one of them.' She shook her head. 'But they live thirty miles away and, what with cooking for the professor and visiting Maureen, I just don't have the time to take Kate to see her friend.'

At a guess, Dizzy would have said the little girl's presence here had something to do with the 'panic' in the kitchen the previous evening.

Poor Kate. She knew herself exactly how traumatic it was to be suddenly separated from your parents, to be taken away from all that was familiar to you. She knew exactly how cruel it could feel, too.

'I could take her, if you like,' she offered decisively.

'Oh, I couldn't let you do a thing like that!' The cook looked shocked at the suggestion. 'You're a guest of the professor's, and——'

'Actually, I'm a guest of his niece,' Dizzy corrected drily, sure that Zach wouldn't like his staff to think *he* had invited her to stay. 'And I have to go into town today, anyway.' The thought of several more days without pilchards was too terrible to contemplate! 'So a few more miles on my journey isn't going to make that much difference. As long as you don't mind trusting Kate to my care, Mrs——' She looked at the older woman enquiringly.

'Mrs Scott,' the cook instantly supplied, looking embarrassed. 'I am sorry, I should have introduced myself sooner. It's just——'

'I understand,' she assured her gently. 'It can't have been easy for you, suddenly having a—five-year-old?—thrust upon you.'

Mrs Scott nodded at the age-guess. 'My job here doesn't leave me too much time for visiting my family. Don't get me wrong,' she added hastily. 'I'm not complaining. Work was what kept me going after my husband died, and Maureen had already had a home of her own for several years. But it means I perhaps haven't spent as much time with little Kate as I should have done, and she's finding it all a bit strange here now that her mother is poorly.'

'Of course she is.' Dizzy sympathised with the whole situation. 'How about if I suggest taking Kate out with me today? You never know, she might have forgotten all about Melissa after we've done some shopping together.'

The cook didn't looked convinced of that. 'It's worth a try, I suppose. As long as you're sure you don't mind?' she added anxiously. She was a small, plump lady with pepper-coloured curly hair, and eyes as blue as Kate's.

'I'm sure,' Dizzy smiled encouragingly, standing up. 'I'll go and talk to Kate while you finish preparing the professor's breakfast. That is his bacon you have out to cook, isn't it?' she prompted teasingly.

'Oh, my goodness, yes!' Mrs Scott gave a frantic glance at the kitchen clock. 'He'll be back any moment, and here's me, not even started cooking!' She hastily got up and moved to the cooker.

Dizzy could see that the other woman had enough to do without the extra worry about her granddaughter, and she went off in search of the little girl. It wasn't all that difficult to find her, the gentle sobs were easily discernible through the partially opened bedroom door.

The staff's quarters were at the back of the wing, and Kate seemed to be sharing a room with her grandmother, a cot-bed having been brought in and put next to the single bed for her.

She looked so small and defenceless as she lay curled up in a ball of misery on the cot-bed, her face wet with tears again.

'Kate,' Dizzy sat down next to her, gently smoothing back the dark tangle of her hair, 'would you like to go out with me today?'

Wide blue eyes were turned to her. 'To go and get Melissa?' she suggested hopefully, still sobbing gently.

'I have some shopping to do first—but afterwards we could go and see Melissa,' she quickly added, as the small face began to crumple.

Kate frowned, wiping away her tears with the back of her hand. 'Why can't she come back with us?'

There was a possibility that Kate would be going home with her father when he returned tomorrow, but there was also the possibility that, between his job and visiting his wife in hospital, Kate's father might think it best if she stayed on with her grandmother for the moment. If that were to happen, it wouldn't do to lead Kate to believe she could see her friend any time she wanted to.

'Don't you think she would miss her home if she did that?' Dizzy said softly. 'And her Mummy and Daddy would miss her if she came to stay with you.'

'But she doesn't have a Mummy and Daddy.' Kate's frown deepened.

Dizzy had to admit to feeling a little puzzled herself. Unless... 'Kate,' she said slowly, 'who *is* Melissa?'

'I told you, she's my friend.' Kate was becoming agitated now.

'Is she a big friend or a little friend?' Dizzy persisted.

'A little friend, of course,' Kate dismissed impatiently, as if she found the question an extremely silly one.

'Does she have blonde hair or black?' Dizzy encouraged.

Kate looked at her consideringly. 'It's the same colour as yours,' she decided. 'Not as long, but Melissa is awful pretty,' she defended with that endearing lisp.

'And are her eyes blue or brown?' With each answer she received, Dizzy became more and more convinced she was right about Melissa.

'Blue, of course.' Kate was really tiring of all these questions now. 'All my dollies have blue eyes,' she reported in a grown-up voice, as if Dizzy ought to have already known that.

Dizzy hugged the little girl impulsively. A doll, of course Melissa had to be a doll. Children missed their friends when they were away from them, but they didn't wake up in the night calling for them! She should have realised sooner, should have known Kate's behaviour was much more serious than being away from a playmate; with her mother in hospital and her father away, the doll had become Kate's one security. It was obviously the doll the little girl usually took to bed with her. She had forgotten about it until she realised it wasn't there, and had woken from sleep when she realised that.

It was all so reminiscent of what had happened to Dizzy when she had been sent away to school, only in her case it had been a tattered, old, lop-eared, cuddly toy rabbit that she had had since she was a baby. When her things were unpacked at school, she found that the rabbit hadn't been included, and had written to her father, asking him to send it on to her. And written to him. And written to him. For a whole term she had dutifully written to him every Sunday, always adding the request about the rabbit at the end of the letter. It wasn't until she went home for Christmas that she managed to sneak Snuggles back to school in her suitcase. For fourteen long weeks she had cried herself to sleep every night, because her father ignored her request for her childhood friend.

Her arms tightened about Kate as she realised the suffering the little girl had gone through without the security of her doll, although she knew Kate's suffering hadn't been deliberate, as hers had, that Melissa had just genuinely been overlooked in the panic of yesterday.

'We'll go and get Melissa after breakfast,' she told the little girl emotionally.

'We will?' Kate pulled back slightly, her eyes wide.

'We will,' she nodded, feeling tearful herself at how easy it had been to allay Kate's suffering—and how easily her own father had found it to ignore her pain. When he had at last found out what she had done that Christmas, he had demanded the return of the rabbit, and told her she was too old for cuddly toys. Maybe she was, but Snuggles wasn't just a cuddly toy to her, he was so much more. For the first time in her life she had told her father a lie, had told him she had lost the rabbit. It had satisfied him, and she got to keep the one thing she truly loved at the time, but the guilt of that lie lay in the bottom of her backpack upstairs...

'Mummy was in too much pain to think of Melissa yesterday, pet,' she comforted the child in her arms. 'And Nanny didn't know about how important Melissa is to you. Now let's wash your face,' she smiled, gently touching the silken cheeks. 'And then you can go and eat some breakfast with Nanny before we go and get Melissa.'

Kate scrambled off the bed, hesitating as she reached the door. 'We really will go and get Melissa?'

Dizzy swallowed hard. 'We really will.'

'Oh, great!' Kate bounced out of the room, wriggling impatiently as her face was washed, eager to get the business of eating breakfast over so that they might leave. 'I can take Melissa with me this afternoon when we go to see Mummy,' she was telling Dizzy as they entered the kitchen a few minutes later.

The kitchen smelt of cooked breakfast, and was noticeably empty of food, so Dizzy could only assume that Zach was now in the dining-room, eating his breakfast. She hoped he didn't disappear into his office too quickly, for she wanted Christi to ask him for the use of a car so that they could go and get Kate's doll.

Mrs Scott looked relieved to see her grand-daughter obediently sit down and begin to eat the toast she had abandoned earlier, although she frowned a little at the mention of Melissa going to the hospital with them.

'A blue-eyed, blonde haired doll,' Dizzy explained in an aside.

'A doll!' the cook predictably gasped.

'Not just any doll,' Dizzy told her softly. 'A very special friend of Kate's.'

'I understand.' Mrs Scott looked thankful that *that* worry, at least, was over. 'I had no idea...'

'Of course you didn't.' Dizzy squeezed her arm understandingly. 'Kate and I plan to go and get her after breakfast,' she added.

'I don't know how to thank you,' the cook said warmly. 'You don't even know Kate and me, and yet you——' She broke off as a bell rang in the room. 'That will be the professor, wanting his second pot of coffee. I really am grateful, Miss James——'

'Dizzy,' she invited smoothly, laughing softly as the other woman frowned. 'It really is my name,' she said derisively. 'See you after breakfast, Kate.' She lightly touched the little girl's shoulder on her way to the door. 'Make sure you eat it all up.'

Kate nodded eagerly, her mouth stuffed full of the toast she had refused to eat earlier.

Dizzy was still smiling as she left the room, although she sobered as she remembered why she had been in this part of the house in the first place, and returned briefly to the kitchen doorway. 'The library?' she prompted, as Mrs Scott turned to her enquiringly.

'Down the corridor and turn right, you can't miss it,' she smiled, picking up the coffee-pot to take through to the professor.

Dizzy wished she *could* miss it, wished she didn't have to put herself through this. But it was inevitable.

It was a beautiful room, a deep red carpet adding a richness to the book-lined room, a fire lit invitingly in the hearth.

Over the fireplace hung the painting she had come here to see, and she reluctantly raised her gaze from the orange and yellow flames, gasping as raw pain ripped through her.

CHAPTER FIVE

THE background of the painting looked harmless enough. It was a children's playroom, with every conceivable toy you could think of or imagine either on the thickly carpeted floor or along the shelved walls. It was like an Aladdin's cave, paradise for any child.

But not for the child who stood to the right of the foreground as she gazed out of the window before her, the toys obviously meaning nothing to her, her expression one of cold uninterest.

She was a child of about seven, neat black patent shoes on her feet, her socks pristine white, not a fold of the pink dress and white over-pinafore out of place, her hair tamed into plaits that lay over each shoulder.

'Perhaps you find this Sherman more to your liking?'

Zach's habit of catching her unawares was becoming too disturbing by half. Especially now. How could she turn and face him when—— She *had* to turn and face him, she admonished herself, straightening her spine, clearing her face of all expression as she slowly turned.

He was wearing an equally comfortable and ill-fitting pair of corduroys as he had yesterday, black this time, coupled with a blue jumper that actually revealed the powerful muscles beneath. It was already warm outside, but inside there was still a chill in the air, although not enough for Zach to wear the baggy jacket that yesterday had so successfully concealed how masculine he was.

With her defences already down, his blatant masculinity was the last thing Dizzy needed just now!

She drew in a ragged breath. 'Is this a Sherman, too?' She pretended surprise, evading a direct answer concerning her feelings for the painting, as she had initially last night about the one of Knollsley Hall.

Zach nodded. 'I told you I had others of hers.' He came further into the room, looking up at the painting appreciatively. 'This is one of her best, I think.'

Dizzy's brows rose. 'A poor-little-rich-girl too bored to play with her toys?' she taunted.

He turned to her slowly, frowning slightly. 'Is that the way you see the painting?'

Defiant colour burnt her cheeks. 'Isn't that exactly what it is?' she challenged, her body held in a defensive stance.

He slowly shook his head. 'Not to me.'

Dizzy shrugged. 'I'm sure I read somewhere that the critics disliked this painting because it lacked emotion.'

'It's full of emotion,' he contradicted impatiently. 'Look at the eyes.' He moved to stand just below the painting. 'Can't you see the suggestion of tears in their depths? Look at the mouth,' he instructed again. 'There's vulnerability beneath the stubbornness. The title of it should tell you that it's a painting of emotion. "Lost Child",' he supplied, as she raised her brows questioningly.

She knew the title of the painting, had seen photographs of it, although never the original before. Zach was right, there *were* tears in the green eyes, and the mouth *did* look as if it trembled on the verge of tears.

But it was all a sham. Her mother had never seen her like that, had already been out of her life for three years by the time she was seven. Oh, the child was definitely her, but she had never had a playroom like this one, and the emotions were purely her mother's, a spoilt child of a woman who found herself in a marriage where she could have everything—like the child in the painting with her toys—except the freedom that lay beyond that window!

Knollsley Hall had become like a prison to Valerie Sherman for the five years she was married to Martin Ellington-James, and by the time Dizzy was four she hadn't been able to stand the restrictions being a politician's wife put on her any longer. She had gone out shopping one day, and just not come back.

Dizzy hadn't been able to believe her mother's desertion of her, had felt sure she was coming back one day. Her father told her he wouldn't take her mother back, even if she came crawling to him on her knees, but, even so, Dizzy had hoped. She had never seen her mother again after that day, just after her fourth birthday.

But she had seen photographs of this painting, had hated her mother anew for using her to depict her own emotions. Last night, Christi had told her that her uncle had the original of the painting, and although she hated the thought of it, Dizzy had always made a point of not running away from anything. But she couldn't run away from the pain of disillusionment this painting evoked even if she had wanted to, it was something that was always with her, had shaped her into the woman she was today. The fact that Zach saw the pain inside the child in the painting only made it worse, as if he had once again pierced the shield she had over her emotions.

'She doesn't look very lost to me,' Dizzy answered him in a hard voice. 'Unless it's among all those toys,' she dismissed coldly. 'Now, if you'll excuse me, I have to go and see Christi.' She couldn't get out of the room, away from Zach, fast enough!

'Dizzy?' He stopped her at the door.

She kept her gaze averted from the painting as she turned to look at him, knowing that although the books tempted her, she would probably never be able to return to this room during the rest of her stay here. 'Yes?' she prompted abruptly.

He looked puzzled by her behaviour, and Dizzy was easily able to guess why. All this emotionalism wasn't really in character with the woman who gave her body at a glance from soulful brown eyes! Well, damn him, she couldn't *be* the clown when she felt as if her soul had been stripped bare!

'If you still want to go into town today, I can have a car put at your disposal,' he offered gruffly.

She relaxed slightly. 'Assuming I can drive, of course,' she drawled.

'I'm sure Christi would be only too happy to accompany you,' he told her distantly.

'I would have thought you would have wanted to keep her away from me as much as possible,' she taunted.

'Dizzy——'

'Sorry.' She held up her hands defensively, knowing she was being unfair, that his reactions had all been to the type of woman he was supposed to believe her to be, although if that were so it made some of his behaviour the night before a little difficult to explain! 'I would appreciate the use of a car.' Especially as that was why she had been going in search of Christi! 'And I'll invite Christi to go with me, if that's all right with you.'

Golden eyes widened. 'Christi is an adult, completely capable of making her own decisions.'

'Yes, but——' She broke off awkwardly.

Zach looked at her consideringly. 'Yes?'

She shrugged, realising how close she had come to ruining everything for Christi with the casual remark that she was hardly likely to want to upset her uncle in the circumstances. No doubt, if Zach knew she was aware of the conditions of Christi's parents' will, he would think her visit here now more than timely!

'Christi and I were never that close,' she dismissed. 'And you've made it very clear you disapprove of me as a companion for her.'

He stiffened. 'As I said, Christi is an adult, capable of making her own decisions about people.'

'OK,' she shrugged. 'I'll ask her and see what she says.'

'You do that,' he invited tersely. 'And eat some breakfast before you leave.'

'Yes, sir,' she returned impishly.

He gave a rueful smile, looking years younger. 'Please,' he added drily. 'I'm sorry we can't accommodate you with pilchards, but . . .'

Dizzy chuckled. 'I think I'll go and find Christi.' She was still smiling as she left the room, Zach's humour a pleasant surprise. Obviously the sternly disapproving expression was as deceptive of his real character as the ill-fitting clothes were of the body that lay beneath them. And with that thought she couldn't help wondering if he would be skinny-dipping again this afternoon . . .

'Only you, Dizzy,' Christi said affectionately, glancing indulgently at the back of the car, where Kate sat cuddling Melissa as if she would never let her go again. 'Most people would have just bought her another doll, instead of driving out to get this one.'

Dizzy shook her head, her gaze on the road ahead as she drove the station-wagon. 'It wouldn't have been the same.'

'Obviously.' Christi smiled at the ecstatic Kate before settling back into her seat. 'But most people wouldn't have cared.'

'Don't make me out to be some sort of heroine, Christi,' she dismissed. 'It will simply be quieter, and your uncle will get his dinner on time in future, now that Kate has her doll.'

'This is Christi, Dizzy,' she reminded gently. 'And I know exactly how hard you aren't!'

She sighed, some of the tension leaving her body. 'I saw the painting, Christi. It's all right,' she ruefully assured, as Christi glanced anxiously into the back of the car. 'Kate's fallen asleep. Apparently she was awake most of the night, crying for her doll.' And, like the little angel she was, she had fallen into an exhausted sleep now that she had her beloved doll back.

'Little love,' Christi murmured indulgently before straightening in her seat, her face full of concern as she looked at Dizzy. 'I thought you probably would have seen the painting by now, but I didn't know how to bring the subject up,' she grimaced.

'You haven't heard the worst of it,' she frowned. 'Your uncle walked in while I was looking at it.'

'Oh, lord,' Christi groaned. 'Did he realise the little girl was you?' Her eyes were wide.

'She isn't me,' Dizzy grated with feeling. 'She's a figment of my mother's—Valerie Sherman's,' she amended tightly, 'imagination.'

Christi gave her a sideways glance. 'You've still made no effort to see her?'

'Why should I want to see her?' she dismissed coldly.

Christi shrugged. 'She is your mother.'

'You know,' Dizzy said thoughtfully, her eyes pained, 'I think your uncle may be right about it sometimes being kinder to be cruel. I know I would have found it easier to understand—and accept— if my father had told me my mother had died and wasn't coming back, rather than the truth, that she just couldn't stand living with either of us any more!' Even now, all these years later, she couldn't keep the bitterness out of her voice.

'I'm sure that can't be the way it happened, Dizzy——'

'What other explanation do you give for her walking out and leaving me with the monster I called Father?' she attacked, her hands tensely clutching the steering wheel, her gaze fixed firmly ahead.

'None,' Christi sighed defeatedly.

'And to think the great British public go out at election time and vote for him in their thousands.' Dizzy shook her head. 'The wonder of it is, he's actually *good* at being an MP; there's even talk of him being successful when the leadership of the party comes up again.'

'Maybe you should write one of those exposé books like all the other kids of famous... Maybe you shouldn't!' Christi backed down ruefully as Dizzy looked at her with raised brows. 'As you say, he's very capable when it comes to his job,' she added hastily. 'It's just that at being a father he falls flat on his face!'

Dizzy's attention returned to the road. 'Not every parent can love their child,' she said flatly.

'How can a father help but love a child like that?' Christi looked affectionately at the sleeping Kate in the back of the car. 'And you were much cuter as a little girl: lovely blonde curls, big green eyes, and freckles,' she defended.

Dizzy self-consciously touched the golden freckles that covered the bridge of her nose today. 'Suffice it to say, my father found it impossible to love me,' she dismissed without emotion. She didn't know how it was possible to feel that way about your own child, either, especially when that child loved you so unquestioningly, but she had come to terms years ago with the fact that *her* father totally rejected her love.

Christi leant her ebony head against the head-rest. 'I think that's partly why I'm so particular when it comes to the man I'm going to marry,' she remarked thoughtfully. 'You really have to care about the same things, want the same things, or you just end up hurting people besides yourselves.'

Dizzy gave her a smile of affection. 'Maybe you should get your dates to fill out a questionnaire before you even consider going out with them!'

'Or put an advertisement in a newspaper stating my own likes and dislikes, and the things I would like in the man I fall in love with,' Christi laughed, easily falling in with the teasing, relieved that the tension of the conversation had passed.

Dizzy's eyes widened. 'Can you do things like that? I thought it was only certain magazines that—well——'

'Not *those* sort of things!' Christi giggled. 'And I'm sure there must be some respectable publication that could deal with it. Although,' she frowned thoughtfully, 'I can't say I've ever seen one,' she admitted disappointedly.

Dizzy gave her friend a rueful smile. 'Wouldn't it be easier to go to one of those dating agencies, where they feed all the relevant information into a computer, and——'

'And come up with the man most compatible to you that they have on their files?' Christi finished disgustedly. 'Advertising in a magazine would be better,' she said, having shaken her head. 'It would reach a much wider audience. If you chose your publication wisely, of course.'

'*Playboy?*' Dizzy arched innocent brows.

'Certainly not,' her friend said indignantly. 'Can you imagine the sort of replies you would get from an advertisement in *there*?'

Laughter glowed in Dizzy's eyes. 'Might be interesting to find out,' she said mischievously.

'Wouldn't it just?' Christi agreed with anticipation. 'Seriously, though, Dizzy——'

'I've always had an aversion to conversations that begin, "seriously, Dizzy",' she winced.

Christi gave her a chiding look. 'You won't sidetrack me with your flippancy,' she warned. 'Your friends, all of us, are worried about you. I mean, talk about the sublime to the ridiculous!' she added ruefully. '*I* have too many boyfriends, and *you* steer clear of having any!'

Ordinarily, Dizzy would have been able to fence off this conversation with comments like she 'had yet to find a man that interested her to that extreme', or she 'was perfectly happy with her life the way that it was'. But since coming to Castle Haven she wasn't sure either of those comments was true any more. She found Zach Bennett not only interesting but exciting, physically and mentally, and with that awareness had come a certain dissatisfaction with the emptiness of her life. Because she wasn't comfortable with any of those emotions, she kept putting off thinking about them, which was a little difficult when she was seeing so much of Zach.

She smiled brightly as she saw Christi watching her curiously, hoping to divert her friend's attention, but knowing she had failed when Christi turned in her seat determinedly.

'Or are you still?' she pounced. 'Tell me, Dizzy, is there someone in London?'

'No,' she answered with some relief.

'New York?'

'No.'

'Toronto?' Christi persisted.

'No,' she laughed.

Her friend's mouth set stubbornly. *'Anywhere?'* she said desperately.

She hesitated only briefly over the fourth denial, but she could see by the speculative gleam in Christi's eyes that she had noticed it—and was relishing it! 'It's nothing serious, Christi——'

'Just having you admit to being *interested* in someone is serious,' Christi refuted. 'Who is he? What does he do? Are you——'

'Enough,' Dizzy cut in laughingly. 'It really isn't anything,' she dismissed lightly. 'I've only *noticed* him. It certainly hasn't been reciprocated, in that way, at least,' she added ruefully, remembering just how Zach was being led to think about her!

'Oh,' Christi looked disappointed. 'Although the fact that you *have* noticed him is something.' She brightened a little. 'It's all right having all these godchildren, Dizzy,' she reproved. 'But you need children of your own.'

'I've barely noticed the man, and you have me married off with children!' she spluttered indignantly. 'Remind me never to confide in you again,' she said disgustedly. 'When *you* manage to find Mr Right, maybe I'll start thinking about it. In the meantime, concentrate on your own lovelife,' she advised firmly.

'Spoilsport!' Christi pouted.

She couldn't help smiling. 'Remember, once you fall in love, I'll start thinking about it,' she teased softly.

'You make me sound so fickle,' Christi sulked. 'There's a man out there for me somewhere, I just have to go out and find him. Once this inheritance nonsense is out of the way, and my career is firmly established, I'm going to do just that!' she announced defiantly.

Dizzy grinned. 'That gives me at least a couple of years, then!'

'Very funny,' her friend derided with sarcasm. 'You never know, I could finish Drama School and walk straight out into a wonderful part that gives me instant stardom!'

'I hope you do, love,' Dizzy told her with quiet sincerity. 'I know how hard you've worked for it, how difficult it was to make the change into acting in the first place.'

'Mummy and Daddy would have been proud of me,' Christi said quietly.

They would have, too. Michael and Diana Bennett had believed that life was to be lived the way you wanted it to be, not the way society decided it should. Having spent more of her formative years with the happy couple than with her own father, she had quickly come to learn that their philosophy on life was a true one: be true to yourself and others. Michael and Diana would have been pleased that Christi was doing what she really felt was right for her.

'Let's not get maudlin,' Christi announced into the sudden silence that had fallen over the car, as they both indulged in affectionate memories of her parents. 'Kate has her doll back, you have a secret love——'

'He isn't secret——' She broke off her indignant denial as she saw the teasing in Christi's eyes. 'Remind me never to play poker with you,' she muttered ruefully.

'*I* don't happen to know any illegal gambling clubs,' Christi announced innocently.

'You introduced me to Jason in the first place,' Dizzy reminded her indignantly.

'He never took *me* to illegal gambling clubs. Come to think of it,' she frowned, '*why* didn't he?'

'Probably because he knows you can't keep a secret,' Dizzy teased.

'You would be surprised,' her friend announced haughtily.

She gave her an indulgent smile. 'I would?'

'Yes.' Christi turned to her eagerly. 'There's something about——' She broke off as she saw Dizzy's teasing expression. 'You tricked me!' she accused.

Dizzy laughed softly. 'Only a little.'

'Well, don't,' her friend complained. 'Uncle Zach would be furious if he realised that *I* know, let alone that I've told anyone else!'

Dizzy had tensed just at the mention of Zach's name, and now that she realised Christi had been about to confide something about him she wished she hadn't teased her about it. She had a burning curiosity to know all there was to know about Zachariah Bennett.

One thing she did know about him: it was almost two-thirty, the usual time Christi had said her uncle went off to do his bird-watching. It was hotter today than it had been yesterday, and she didn't doubt that Zach was once again at the lake, indulging in a naked swim . . .

CHAPTER SIX

'JUST what sort of unfeeling monster do the two of you think I am?'

Dizzy and Christi both looked up with a start as Zach strode furiously into the lounge where they were both waiting for him before dinner.

It was the first time Dizzy had seen him since their conversation in the library that morning, having used a walk with Christi this afternoon to keep herself from the magnetic pull going to the lake to watch Zach had for her.

As far as she knew, Christi hadn't seen her uncle since this morning, either, and from the puzzled look her friend was shooting her she had no more idea of the reason for Zach's anger than Dizzy did.

Her gaze returned to Zach, loving the springy softness of his hair as it dried in the loose waves even the shortness of the style wasn't able to deter. Once again he wore the black evening suit and a white shirt, and once again his magnificent virility shone above the ill-fitting clothes. She couldn't understand why Christi wasn't able to see just how attractive he was; he was becoming more and more so to her by the hour!

'What did you think I was going to do when I found out Mrs Scott's daughter had had an emergency operation and that her granddaughter was staying here with her?' he rasped at their puzzled expressions. 'Throw them both out into the street?'

Christi's face cleared, and she turned to give Dizzy a rueful grimace before answering her uncle. 'Of course not, Uncle Zach,' she soothed. 'Mrs Scott seemed to be handling the situation, and I— we, believed Fredericks would have told you about it if he believed it was important,' she added triumphantly as the thought obviously just occurred to her.

Zach didn't look impressed by the claim. 'Fredericks obviously *didn't* feel it was important,' he bit out abruptly. 'But Mrs Scott is full of the fact that my niece and Miss James have been taking care of her granddaughter for her today, that the two of you even drove thirty miles to Kate's home so that she could be reunited with her favourite doll!'

'That was——'

'—Christi's idea,' Dizzy put in softly, shooting her friend a silencing look as she gave a sudden frown. 'A very thoughtful and kind one, considering that Kate was so upset about not having the doll with her.' She smiled approvingly at Christi.

'Oh, but——'

'Don't you think so, Zach?' she prompted him, giving Christi another warning glance.

'Very,' he snapped. 'And I'm sure Mrs Scott appreciated it as much as the child did.' His expression softened as he looked at his niece. 'But,' he added in a controlled voice, 'if either of you had taken the trouble to tell me about the domestic difficulty Mrs Scott was having, I would have given *her* the time off to see to her granddaughter and go to the hospital to visit her daughter.'

And it was because they hadn't that he obviously considered they believed him to be 'some sort of monster'!

Since he was Mrs Scott's employer, someone probably should have told him about little Kate. Christi still seemed to be floundering under the surprise of hearing herself described as the 'Good Samaritan', so she wasn't going to be much help in explanations just yet!

'We all managed perfectly well, without having to worry you,' Dizzy placated. 'This way, Christi and I kept busy, Mrs Scott felt free to take care of your needs, knowing her granddaughter was in Christi's more than capable hands——' again Christi frowned at being given the praise for that deed '—and I don't think anyone can doubt Kate's happiness,' she rushed on.

'Probably not,' Zach acknowledged abruptly. 'Is it my imagination, or did "master of my own home" seem to get forgotten among all this organising?' He arched questioning brows.

Dizzy suddenly felt on safer ground, sure that over the years she had become an expert on trying to placate an indignant male. 'You're such a busy person, Zach,' she said warmly. 'None of us wanted to interrupt your work by bothering you with this trivial problem.'

His eyes were cold as he looked at her. 'I doubt Mrs Scott's daughter considered it trivial.'

'No—well——'

'Or Kate last night, as she cried at the strangeness of her surroundings. Or Mrs Scott, as she tried to comfort her,' he bit out with controlled violence.

This wasn't going at all as she had planned; usually she only had to simper and tell her father how important she realised his work was, and he would become so lost in his own self-importance he would forget what the lecture had been about. Obviously Zach was made of much sterner stuff. Or, more likely, he wasn't so full of himself that he didn't have time for other people's feelings. She was sure that both of those things were true about Zach; he wasn't about to be side-tracked by effusive compliments about his work, and he obviously cared for other people very much, as much angered by the misery he might have averted if he had known of Mrs Scott's predicament as he was by the fact that no one had chosen to tell him. She didn't doubt that, if he had known, he would have given Mrs Scott the time off to go and stay with Kate at her own home rather than having the little girl come here, where nothing was familiar to her. No doubt the cook herself would have realised that, if she hadn't been in such a panic after yesterday's emergency.

'It wasn't a deliberate omission on anyone's part, I'm sure,' Dizzy shrugged uncomfortably.

'It was just that no one thought I would be interested!' Zach rasped.

She grimaced. 'Yes. I mean—no. I mean——'

He drew in an impatient breath, turning to his niece. 'Is that what you thought, too?'

Christi frowned. 'I——'

'Of course it isn't,' Dizzy defended, aware that Christi was fast losing ground in her uncle's esteem. 'Christi——'

'—is perfectly able to answer for herself,' Zach finished firmly. 'Do you have anything to say, Christi?' His voice softened a little as he spoke to her.

Her head went back. 'Yes, I do.' She looked at Dizzy before turning back to her uncle. 'We didn't commit any crime, Uncle Zach, unless it was by omission,' she defended firmly. 'At the time, we were more concerned with Kate than your possible hurt feelings.'

Dizzy stared at her friend in amazement. She didn't need anyone to tell her what was happening, after all the years she had known Christi she knew that, although slow to anger, when Christi reached a saturation point she nevertheless bubbled over. And she was fast approaching that point when it came to impressing her uncle with her maturity and kindness. Dizzy was aware that taking the credit for collecting Kate's doll had probably contributed to it; although Christi didn't mind having a little fun at her uncle's expense, she found the subject of Kate's distress too serious to be played around with.

So did she! But thoughtfulness towards a child hardly fitted in with the selfish drifter she was supposed to be!

Zach looked slightly taken aback by the attack, gently made as it was, and then his expression softened. 'You're right,' he sighed. 'The important thing is that the situation has been resolved to everyone's satisfaction. And Kate was definitely looking bright enough when I saw her in the kitchen just now,' he added indulgently.

'I knew you would understand, Uncle Zach.' Christi gave him a spontaneous hug, grinning up at him affectionately as she pulled back.

Dizzy watched with longing as Christi did easily what she had longed to do since the moment she had first seen Zach, what she had also been fighting against in an agony of doubt and confusion.

Over the years she had chosen her friends well, felt able to relax and share affection with them, but falling in love with a man was a different matter altogether, involved a commitment she had sworn never to make to any man. These feelings she had, to lose herself in Zach's arms, were as frightening as they were unsettling.

'Speaking of kitchens,' he was telling Christi now, 'as I've given Mrs Scott the rest of the evening off so that she can spend it with Kate, we have the little problem of who is to serve up the supper she has left prepared for us. I thought the two of you could do it,' he told them blandly.

The two women burst out laughing at his totally innocent expression, Christi hugging him again.

'You're just a big softie, after all,' she chuckled indulgently.

Blond brows rose over honey-brown eyes. 'Did you have some reason to suppose I wasn't?'

'No, of course not,' Christi denied instantly. 'Come on, Dizzy,' she added briskly. 'Let's go and see to the food before it spoils.'

Mrs Scott might have been given the evening off by her employer, but she hadn't gone until the soup, chicken dinner and dessert had been prepared. There was little for Dizzy and Christi to do except

Discover deliciously different romance with 4 Free Novels from

Harlequin Presents®

Sit back and enjoy four exciting romances—yours **FREE** from Harlequin Reader Service! But wait . . . there's *even more* to this great offer!

A Useful, Practical Digital Clock/Calendar—FREE

As a free gift simply to thank you for accepting four free books we'll send you a stylish digital quartz clock/calendar—a handsome addition to any decor! The changeable, month-at-a-glance calendar pops out, and may be replaced with a favorite photograph.

PLUS A FREE MYSTERY GIFT—a surprise bonus that will delight you!

All this just for trying our Reader Service!

MONEY-SAVING HOME DELIVERY

Once you receive 4 FREE books and gifts, you'll be able to preview more great romance reading in the convenience of your own home at less than retail prices. Every month we'll deliver 8 brand-new Harlequin Presents novels right to your door months before they appear in stores. If you decide to keep them, they'll be yours for only $2.24 each! That's 26¢ less per book than the retail price—plus 89¢ postage and handling per shipment. And you may cancel at any time, for any reason, and still keep your free books and gifts, just by dropping us a line!

BE TEMPTED! COMPLETE, DETACH AND MAIL YOUR POSTPAID ORDER CARD TODAY AND RECEIVE 4 FREE BOOKS, A DIGITAL CLOCK/CALENDAR AND MYSTERY GIFT—PLUS LOTS MORE!

A FREE
Digital Clock/Calendar
and Mystery Gift *await you, too!*

Harlequin Presents®

Harlequin Reader Service®
P.O. Box 609, Fort Erie, Ontario L2A 9Z9

☐ **YES!** Please rush me my four Harlequin Presents novels with my FREE Digital Clock/Calendar and Mystery Gift. As explained on the opposite page, I understand that I am under no obligation to purchase any books. The free books and gifts remain mine to keep.

308 CIH U1C8

NAME _____
(please print)

ADDRESS _____ APT. _____

CITY _____ PROVINCE _____ POSTAL CODE _____

Offer limited to one per household and not valid to current Presents subscribers.
Prices subject to change.

Business Reply Mail

No Postage Stamp
Necessary if Mailed
in Canada

Postage will be paid by

Harlequin Reader Service
P.O. Box 609
Fort Erie, Ontario
L2A 9Z9

Canada Post
Postes Canada
125

Clip and mail this personal card today!

put the food into the vegetable dishes, ready for Fredericks to bring into the dining-room for them.

'That was a close thing,' Dizzy remarked as she strained the vegetables over the sink. 'I thought you were going to lose your temper just now,' she explained at Christi's questioning look.

'So did I,' her friend grimaced. 'I know why you gave me the credit about Kate's doll.' She held up her hands defensively. 'But I wasn't comfortable with it; I suddenly wasn't comfortable with the whole situation,' she admitted ruefully. 'Uncle Zach's a strange one.' She shook her head. 'I just think I have him taped, and he shows me yet another side of his character.'

'He was certainly angry at not being told about Mrs Scott's daughter,' Dizzy replied noncommittally, not willing to get into a discussion about how fascinating *she* found the different facets of Zach's nature!

Christi grinned. 'Not so angry he couldn't make a joke about giving us this work to do.' She placed the last of the serving bowls in the food warmer. 'I know one thing,' she announced with satisfaction as they left the kitchen together. 'I've certainly been proven correct about there never being a dull moment when you're about! So far we've spent the day chasing after a doll, taken over the castle kitchen for the evening, and you've had the *strangest* effect on——'

'Yes?' Dizzy prompted sharply as she broke off abruptly, Christi's eyes wide as she looked at her as if she had never seen her before. 'Christi!' she prompted with suspicion. 'What is it?'

Christi gave a start of surprise at having her train of thought interrupted, shaking her head as she gave a sudden, overly bright smile. 'Nothing,' she dismissed, a little too lightly for Dizzy's peace of mind. 'Shall we rejoin my uncle?'

Dizzy didn't like it when Christi became secretive; it usually meant she was up to something. 'Christi,' she began warningly, 'you——'

'Fredericks is ready to serve the soup,' her friend prompted, as the butler appeared in the corridor behind them with the tureen.

Dizzy gave her a look that promised this wasn't the end of the subject. Her uneasiness increased as Christi seemed to be watching her closely through dinner.

She deliberately kept her conversation light, although she noticed that Christi stayed pretty much out of that, too, leaving it up to Dizzy and Zach to keep the conversation flowing.

By the end of the meal, Dizzy was feeling decidedly uneasy by Christi's preoccupied expression. Her friend was plotting something, and this time she wanted to know what it was before she was thrown *into* the situation.

'I don't know what you're talking about,' Christi denied, after Dizzy had followed her to her bedroom and demanded to know what was going on.

'Christi——'

'It was pretty decent of Uncle Zach to help with the washing up like that,' Christi commented as she unzipped her dress.

It had been a little too cosy in the kitchen, with the three of them doing the washing up, for Dizzy's peace of mind, but she had to agree that it had been a pleasant surprise when Zach had offered to help them. If it had been *her* father in that situation, he wouldn't have given Mrs Scott the evening off in the first place, let alone helped do some of the work.

But she hadn't needed Zach's show of kindness to know he was nothing like her father, she had known that instinctively. It was the commitment of a relationship that she feared, rather than the man himself.

Her father hadn't remarried after his divorce from her mother, and when she was older Dizzy had secretly wondered if that weren't because the role of a wronged man who had never got over the loss of his wife was considered rather appealing to the electorate. Maybe she was being unfair to him because of her own feelings of resentment towards him, but she had known he hadn't felt her mother's betrayal enough not to have had a succession of quietly discreet affairs over the years. As for her mother, if newspaper reports of her life were to be believed, each successive lover was younger than the last. They would soon be younger than Dizzy herself!

Being brought up in a background like that didn't make for a trust in everlasting love. Even the happy marriages of several of her friends could not change years of mistrusting the sort of love that left one open to pain and disillusionment.

Knowing how close she was to feeling that sort of love for Zach Bennett, she should be running away from here as fast as her legs would carry her.

But instead she stayed, and it wasn't just for Christi's benefit, either.

'Very nice of him,' she answered Christi's comment. 'But stop changing the subject and tell me what you're plotting in that devious little mind of yours.'

Christi gave a pained frown. 'I think I take exception to the "little" part of that.'

'You're up to something.' Dizzy wasn't to be diverted. 'And I want to know what it is!'

She wasn't at all reassured by Christi's look of pained innocence at the accusation.

'All right.' She dropped the act as Dizzy simply continued to look at her. 'But I'm not up to anything, or planning anything. In fact, this development could completely ruin everything for me,' she added ruefully, but without too much real distress, as if the price she had to pay was worth it.

Dizzy tensed, looking at her friend warily. 'What do you mean?'

Christi's face was full of affection, her blue eyes softened with love. 'You and Uncle Zach are so aware of each other, the air simply crackled with it tonight at dinner,' she said softly.

Fiery colour burnt Dizzy's cheeks. 'What nonsense!' she finally managed to splutter. But it wasn't; as she and Zach had talked tonight she had been fully aware of him, and Christi had just confirmed that she hadn't imagined Zach's response to her.

Christi squeezed her hand. 'We can't let him go on thinking those things about you, love——'

'You really are imagining things, Christi.' She deliberately made her voice lightly scoffing. 'The fusty, dusty professor and me!' She shook her head as if Christi had gone slightly insane.

Her friend looked unmoved by the act. 'How long did you continue to think of him as fusty and dusty?' she gently chided.

She never had; how could she when her first sight of him had been as he swam naked only feet away from her?

Her guilty blush gave her away. 'All right, so I don't think of him that way,' she admitted sharply. 'But I don't think of him in connection with husband and children, either! Leave things as they are, Christi, please,' she pleaded.

'Dizzy, would you recognise love if it came up and bit you on the nose?' Christi prompted softly.

'Would *you*?' she attacked, completely on the defensive.

Her friend didn't look in the least offended. 'I've had my moments,' she shrugged. 'Nothing like the electricity flowing between you and Uncle Zach, though,' she said with satisfaction.

'I think you've been reading too many happy-ever-after stories,' Dizzy dismissed. 'Real life just isn't like that.'

'It can be,' Christi told her quietly.

'Not for me!' She strode angrily to the door. 'So please keep your matchmaking efforts to yourself!'

'All right,' her friend shrugged.

'I mean it, Christi.' She was breathing raggedly in her agitation, not trusting Christi's ready agreement one little bit. 'If you try to get your uncle and me together, I'll leave here so fast, you'll have some difficult explanations to make.'

'I said all right,' Christi said irritably, picking up her nightgown and robe, in preparation of taking a shower. 'But the two of you could be good for each—— *All right,*' she snapped frustratedly at Dizzy's furious glare. 'But don't blame me if you're passing up your one chance at love.' She slammed into the adjoining bathroom.

Dizzy left the room slowly, deeply disturbed. The last thing she would have wished for was that Christi would realise her awareness of Zach. Or accuse him of being equally aware of her! Was that really true? There was an electricity between them, that couldn't be denied, but was Zach really aware of it, too? If he was, she was surprised *he* wasn't the one running away!

Once again she had trouble sleeping after her nightly read, getting up to move restlessly about the room. She had purchased the pilchards today, and a glass of milk and something to nibble on might have helped her to relax enough to sleep, but after her conversation with Christi, and what had happened last night, she was loath to venture downstairs. Her defences were a little dented tonight, and if Zach should come down again . . . She dared not risk it.

Instead, she sat in front of one of the windows and looked out at the mountains and lakes that were clearly visible in the bright moonlight, hoping to gain some relaxation from their soothing presence, but finding the memories of the lake she tried to keep her gaze averted from too disturbing.

How long she had been sitting there when the gentle knock sounded on the door she had no idea, but she knew it had to be very late—or very early, as Zach had pointed out the night before. Damn, he was in her thoughts so much now, she was even starting to refer to his comments and opinions.

She almost fell over with shock when she opened the door to find him standing there!

She had been expecting it to be Christi, believing her friend couldn't sleep either. Instead it was Zach, dressed just as he had been last night, and he was carrying a tray.

He smiled as her gaze rose shyly from the milk and biscuits on the tray to his face. 'I'm afraid I just couldn't bring myself to open the tin of pilchards,' he teased softly, as he carried the tray into the room and placed it on the side of the dressing-table Dizzy quickly cleared. Then he turned to face her, his hands thrust into the pockets of his robe.

'I didn't expect—you didn't have to bring me this.' She shook her head dazedly, even more disturbed by his presence in her bedroom than she had been at being caught in the kitchen last night.

He shrugged. 'I saw a light under your door and, remembering how you couldn't sleep last night...'

She couldn't take this. Her friends were kind, always considerate, but they understood that she needed to be alone sometimes, and they never intruded. No one had *ever* brought her milk and biscuits in bed because they knew she couldn't sleep.

The tears weren't welcome and she cursed them, but she couldn't stop them.

Zach's rueful smile faded as he saw the well of tears she wasn't quick enough to hide, and he looked suddenly alarmed. 'If you really want the pilchards, I could——'

'I don't want the pilchards,' she choked with a watery smile. 'I want—I want——' She looked up at him beseechingly.

He drew in a ragged breath, then took a step towards her, hesitating slightly before his arms came around her and drew her fiercely against him. 'Oh, God, how I've wanted this too!' he groaned into the softness of her fly-away hair. 'Dizzy!' he breathed softly, as if he couldn't believe this was happening.

Dizzy didn't believe it was happening either, their hearts thundering loudly together in the silence of the room, their arms about each other as not even a wisp of air could come between them.

Held against him like this she could feel the hardness of the rippling muscles she had witnessed that first day, knew the strength of him, knew what it felt like to feel cherished, as if she were a fragile butterfly he had to protect.

He captured her chin as she looked up at him, staring deeply into her eyes, flames flickering in the depths of honey-brown. And then his head lowered, and his lips claimed hers.

Dizzy had never been kissed before. Whenever she went out, it was always with a crowd of friends, and the men were always as much friends as the women, treating her like 'one of the boys'. For any of them to think of her in a romantic light would have been laughable. And so, in her twenty-one years, she had never been kissed.

But she was being kissed now, and by a man who knew exactly what he was doing, if the gentle way he pulled lightly on her chin, so that her lips were open to his, was anything to go by!

Pleasure rippled through her body at the gentle movement of his mouth against hers, and she clung to the broadness of his shoulders as the caress deepened.

The kiss went on and on, and she literally *felt* dizzy by the time Zach's mouth moved to her cheek and then down to her throat, nuzzling against the silky skin there as Dizzy quivered with response, her senses heightened to fever-pitch. She had never felt so alive, so—so sensitised, trembling as Zach's hands caressed her back and sides in rhythmic motions.

'Dizzy, I——' Whatever he had been about to say was cut off by the sound of an eerie scream echoing up the stairway and bouncing off the walls.

'Kate!' Dizzy tensed, her face flushed as she pulled out of Zach's arms, unable to meet his gaze as she moved away from him. 'She must have had a nightmare. I—I have to go to her.'

Zach straightened, the flames dying in his eyes, a frown to his brow as if he, too, were puzzled at what had just happened between him and the unwanted guest of his niece. His mouth tightened. 'Of course,' he nodded tersely. 'I'll come down with you.'

'No!' She swallowed hard at the scowl that settled on his brow. 'I—of course you must come down— if you want to.' She moved jerkily to the door, still shaking very badly.

He nodded again. 'I want to,' he bit out.

Dizzy preceded him out of the room, amazed that her legs could support her. She gave a rueful glance at Christi's closed bedroom door; her friend might like to go to bed late, but once she was asleep it would take the house falling down to wake her before she was ready!

She was very conscious of Zach just behind her all the way down the stairs and through to Kate's room. The little girl could be heard sobbing quietly now, and Mrs Scott looked grateful to see Dizzy when she entered after a brief knock, although the poor cook looked more than a little disconcerted when her employer entered the room directly behind Dizzy. Clasping her nightgown to her buxom figure, she put up a self-conscious hand to the rollers in her hair.

'Dizzy!' As soon as Kate saw her she pulled out of her grandmother's arms and launched herself at Dizzy. 'I want my mummy,' she sobbed, her arms tightly clasped about Dizzy's neck.

Dizzy spoke to her softly, reminding her that her mother was in the hospital, getting well again, but that her daddy would be here tomorrow to take care of her.

All the time she spoke to the distressed child she was aware of Zach as he stood across the room. He had come to an abrupt halt in the doorway, as if realising his presence here was more than a little unexpected. He frowned as he watched her holding and soothing Kate.

Mrs Scott had managed to pull on her robe, obviously still uncomfortable with the intimacy of the situation, but doing her best not to show it. 'I hope we didn't wake you both.' She sounded flustered. 'She just woke up screaming,' she apologised lamely.

'It's all very strange for her,' Zach excused softly, his hands thrust into the pockets of his robe, his hair falling rakishly over his forehead in golden waves.

Dizzy blushed as she remembered the way her hands had run through the softness of that hair only minutes earlier. She turned quickly away as she realised he had evaded answering Mrs Scott's query about having woken them, although she doubted it had crossed the other woman's mind that the two of them might have been awake *together*!

Dizzy was doing her best to pretend it had never happened, and she was sure Zach felt the same way about it—that the lateness of the hour and the intimacy of her bedroom had brought about the situation. In future, she would make sure the light didn't show under her door when she lay awake at night!

Kate's sobs quietened as she held her, and she was relieved to see tired lids drooping over the deep blue eyes.

Suddenly Kate jerked herself wide awake, her arms tightening about Dizzy once again. 'Stay with me,' she pleaded brokenly.

'Of course, darling,' she assured her unhesitatingly. 'Nanny and I will both be here.' She looked up as she saw a movement out of the corner of her eye, realising by the tension in Zach's body that he had taken the remark to be a dismissal. And he looked far from pleased about it! She hadn't actually meant it that way, had meant only to reassure Kate, but after what had happened between them a short time ago it would be a relief to have his presence removed. Her head went back defensively. 'I'm sure we can manage here, Professor,' she told him with quiet firmness. 'If you would like to get back to bed...'

He seemed about to say something, and then obviously changed his mind, nodding abruptly. 'But I'd like to see you in the morning, Dizzy.' He spoke softly but, nevertheless, the fact that he would brook no argument to his request was clearly apparent.

She swallowed hard. 'Yes. Of course.'

'In the library. At ten o'clock,' he added precisely.

'Not in the library!' She blushed at the unmistakable vehemence of her tone, although she was relieved to see she hadn't woken Kate. But Zach and Mrs Scott were giving her frowning looks, and she made a concerted effort to relax herself. 'I have a horror of all those books.' She was deliberately flippant. 'I'd prefer to talk over a cup of coffee in the lounge.'

Despite his incongruous appearance, Zach was every inch the professor at the moment, as remote and disapproving as he had been when Christi introduced the two of them the day before yesterday. God, was it really only then? So much seemed to have happened since then.

'Very well,' he agreed distantly. 'Goodnight, ladies,' he added with a slight softening of his expression as he looked at Mrs Scott.

'Oh, dear,' the cook groaned, once she and Dizzy were alone with the sleeping Kate, Dizzy settling the little girl back on the pillows before tucking the bedclothes in around her. 'I hope he isn't too angry about all this.' She looked worried.

Dizzy straightened. 'He isn't angry at all,' she assured with certainty, knowing Zach *wasn't* angry about Kate's having woken up in this way. His feelings concerning what had happened in her bedroom a short time ago were, however, a different matter altogether! No doubt he wanted to see her in the morning so that he could tell her succinctly that he would not appreciate her telling Christi what had taken place between them. He needn't worry about that; telling Christi was the last thing on her mind! 'Now you get some sleep,' she soothed the older woman gently. 'You need your rest after being awake most of last night. I'll just sit with Kate for a while, if you don't mind.'

Mrs Scott looked down lovingly at the angelic little girl, her dark hair splayed out across the pillow as she slept. 'I don't think there's any need now,' she spoke softly. 'I'm sure she'll sleep until morning.'

'I'd like to sit with her for a while, if I'm not intruding?'

'Of course not,' the cook smiled. 'Promises mean so much to children, don't they?' she said understandingly. 'But I think I will just try and snatch a few hours' sleep, if that's all right?'

'I'd rather you did,' she smiled encouragingly. 'I'll just sit beside Kate until I'm sure she's going to stay asleep.'

She knew by the even breathing several minutes later that the exhausted cook had gone back to sleep, relaxing slightly herself now that she didn't have to put on that cheerful act for anybody.

Mrs Scott was right, promises did mean so much to children, and she had had far too many of them broken when she was a child not to appreciate how hurtful it was when an adult let you down. And she had no intention of being guilty of that herself.

Besides, she had no wish to return to her bedroom just yet, for she was hoping that, by the time she did return, her time in Zach's arms would all seem like a dream.

But when she returned to her bedroom several hours later, she knew that it hadn't been. The cold milk and biscuits that stood on her dressing-table reminded her all too vividly that it had really happened.

And a few hours from now she was going to have to face Zach across the lounge and pretend she had been as unaffected by it as he was...

CHAPTER SEVEN

'BUT what does he want to talk to you about?' Christi persisted.

The two of them were eating a late breakfast together and, although Dizzy hadn't relished telling her friend about her appointment with Zach this morning, she had realised it had to be done.

She had told Christi about Kate waking up the night before, how both she and Zach had gone down to investigate, what she hadn't told her friend was that she and Zach had been together in her bedroom when they had heard Kate cry! Without that relevant piece of information, his asking to see her this morning seemed slightly out of context.

'Maybe he's thinking of asking me to take over full-time as cook, while Mrs Scott goes off to take care of her family?' she teased. 'At least I'd be earning my keep!'

'I hate it when you're flippant,' Christi reproved gently.

Dizzy shrugged unconcernedly. 'Well, then, maybe he wants to ask me to leave so that there's one less mouth to cater for.'

'I don't believe that.' Christi shook her head, looking very beautiful in the rich blue sun-dress that perfectly matched the colour of her eyes. Next to her, in her denims and green vest-top, Dizzy felt less attractive than she usually did!

She sipped her coffee. 'Then I'm as much in the dark as you are,' she dismissed, not quite truthfully, for she was sure that last night in her bedroom would enter into the conversation *somewhere*.

Christi chewed on her bottom lip, uncaring of the fact that the act removed her lipgloss. 'Maybe I should have a word with him——'

'No!' Dizzy drew in a steadying breath as Christi looked at her sharply for her outburst. She really would have to calm down, or Christi would have the truth out of her, and then there would be no stopping the other woman from her matchmaking! 'I'm sure it's nothing important,' she said brightly.

Christi gave her a suspicious frown, but she didn't pressure her any further. 'I shall expect a full report when you're through,' she warned, as Dizzy went off to keep her appointment.

She hesitated outside the lounge. She knew Zach was in there, because Mrs Scott had just performed her last duty before she and Kate went off to meet her son-in-law at the airport, the coffee just waiting in the lounge for Dizzy to go in and pour it.

She straightened her shoulders and took a deep breath, before firmly opening the door and entering the room, faltering only slightly as Zach looked up at her without the screen of his glasses to lessen the impact of those beautiful honey-brown eyes.

The baggy tweed jacket was back today, with an open-necked shirt that didn't look as if he had slept in it—something she knew he didn't do, anyway— and a pair of neatly pressed brown trousers. The clothes still didn't fit him that well, but they were an improvement on that first day.

Dizzy's heart skipped a beat as her gaze once more returned to his face, affected as she usually was by the male perfection she found there.

She tensed as he crossed the room towards her, watching him warily as he firmly removed her hand from the door and closed it behind her.

His mouth twisted as he looked down and saw her apprehension. 'Come and sit down, Dizzy,' he invited softly. 'I don't bite. Although perhaps you can't be too sure of that after last night.' His gaze shifted to the lobe of her ear before quickly moving away again.

Dizzy felt a quiver down her spine as she remembered the ecstasy of having him nibble on her earlobe. She hadn't known there could be such pleasure from such a simple act.

'Come and have some coffee,' Zach prompted as he saw her uncertainty, gently touching her arm.

At the first touch of his fingers against her bare flesh she moved into uncoordinated action, almost running across the room to sit on the sofa in front of the coffee tray.

Zach followed more slowly, a deep frown between his eyes. 'Dizzy——'

'Coffee?' she suggested sharply.

He sighed, thrusting his hands into his trouser pockets. 'Maybe it would help ease the tension a little,' he nodded slowly.

Tension? What did he have to feel tense about? Dizzy wondered dazedly. *She* had been the one to turn a simple gesture of friendship into something neither of them were comfortable with. She should have just accepted the tray of milk and biscuits and let Zach go back to his own room, not looked at

him with such longing that he had felt compelled
to take her into his arms!

'Thanks.' He accepted the cup of coffee she
handed him, walking over to the window. He turned
suddenly, as if he had just come to a decision. 'I
realise I owe you an apology for last night,' he bit
out abruptly. 'But, somehow, in the circumstances,
an apology doesn't seem enough.' He looked grim.

Dizzy sat back in puzzled surprise. *He* owed *her*
an apology?

Zach shook his head self-disgustedly. 'You're a
guest in my home,' he rasped. 'I had no right to
take advantage of your situation here.'

Take advantage? She had almost been begging
him to make love to her last night!

'I'm not surprised that you don't feel you have
anything to say to me.' He put his untouched coffee
cup back on the tray with controlled violence. 'I'm
pretty disgusted with myself right now,' he bit out
grimly. 'I can only apologise again, and hope that
you'll believe me when I say it won't happen again.'

Dizzy was still speechless; this was the last thing
she had been expecting when she had kept this
meeting with him this morning. She had thought
it might be somewhere nearer what she had teasingly told Christi: that he wanted to ask her to leave.
She just didn't know what to say.

'That's all I had to say,' Zach told her abruptly,
moving awkwardly to the door. 'Please believe it
won't happen again,' he said again before leaving
the room, closing the door behind him, as if to give
her a few moments' privacy.

She blinked dazedly, realising that during the
whole conversation all she had said was 'Coffee?'.

Zach had apologised for kissing her. He wasn't angry with her, didn't believe she had deliberately encouraged him, as she had been afraid that he would. It was incredible, unbelievable, but he had taken full responsibility for those kisses.

For the first time, she allowed herself to remember what he had said just before he kissed her, how he had 'wanted it, too'. He really had wanted to kiss and caress her, long before last night in her bedroom?

As far as she knew, no man had ever wanted to kiss her before, let alone apologised afterwards for taking advantage of her.

Had Zach *really* wanted it as badly as she had? It put a whole new aspect on their relationship if he had. Zach had been hurt in the past, too, a different sort of hurt, but he had known the pain of losing someone he loved, and stayed away from involvement since that time. But last night he had taken a chance on her, had allowed her to see the emotions behind the man. It was going to be up to her to make the next move. If there was a next move...

'Well?' Christi burst unannounced into the room, her face alight with curiosity. 'Uncle Zach went to his study ages ago. I've been waiting for you to come and tell me what he said!' she complained as she threw herself into the chair opposite Dizzy.

She smiled. 'What were you doing, lurking about in the hallway, waiting for him to leave?'

'Nice. Very nice,' Christi drawled with sarcasm. 'Actually, I was "lurking about" in the dining-room,' she admitted ruefully.

Dizzy chuckled. 'At least you're honest about it.' And she wasn't about to be quite so honest, for if she told Christi the truth there would be no stopping her! 'Your uncle just wanted to check that everything went all right last night with Kate,' she invented lightly.

'Is that all?' Christi looked disappointed. 'I imagined him inviting you out to dinner, at least.'

Dizzy gave her a chiding look. 'Is that very likely?'

Christi grinned. 'Considering the state of our catering situation, yes! He could have offered to take us both out: I don't mind doing breakfast and lunch, but it would have been nice to go out for dinner.'

'For your information, Fredericks has arranged for an agency to send along a cook until Mrs Scott can come back here,' she told her drily.

'I still think Uncle Zach could have taken us both out for dinner,' Christi said wistfully. 'Do you suppose that when the two of you are married he'll let me just call him Zach?' she added with a sideways glance at Dizzy.

After her outrageous suggestions last night, Dizzy was ready for her, and answered calmly, 'When Zach and I are married the sky will be green!'

Christi was unperturbed. 'I mean, I have no intention of calling my best friend "Aunt"!'

Dizzy shook her head. 'You're incorrigible.'

Her friend smiled confidently. 'I'm determined.'

'Christi,' she sobered, 'don't interfere in this, hm?'

'Too important?' her friend prompted gently.

'Too delicate,' she corrected ruefully.

'I don't have to tell you that I wholeheartedly approve of the idea?' Christi told her softly.

'No.' She gave a grateful smile.

'I'll even give him away at the wedding,' Christi joked lightly, although the affection in her eyes belied the teasing.

'He doesn't have to be given away; I do.' She sighed. 'And my father would have done that years ago if he could!'

'I refuse to let you think about *him*,' Christi said firmly, standing up. 'Just remember that none of your friends would ever willingly lose your friendship. Especially me.'

'So you won't do anything to make things awkward for Zach and me?' she prompted beseechingly.

'I'll be the model of decorum,' Christi promised. 'Just don't wait too long, hm?' she grimaced, frustrated at the restraint being put on her impulsive nature.

The lake was even more of a temptation that afternoon, as it was, Dizzy spent most of that time looking out of the window, wishing she could magic away the hill that hid the lake from her view!

Was she really ready for a relationship with Zach? It was the question she had to answer before taking things any further. And she didn't know. She just *didn't know*.

She had never believed there could be anyone for her like Zach. That instant attraction had deepened into liking and respect, into a physical awareness that made her tremble. But her mother must have felt that way about her father once, and look what had happened to that relationship! She was frightened of taking a risk on her emotions, although she was very much afraid it was already too late for that!

'Isn't this nice?' Christi announced with satisfaction, looking at them expectantly.

Despite the fact that the replacement cook had arrived at the castle that afternoon, Christi had still got her way and persuaded her uncle to take them both out to dinner. Walking down the wide stairway to meet Zach had been a little difficult for Dizzy to do after their earlier conversation, but Christi's light chatter had easily covered the moment of awkwardness, the three of them talking lightly together as they drove to the restaurant.

Nevertheless, Dizzy was very aware of Zach as he sat across the table from her, and watched his hands, because heat flooded her cheeks every time she looked into his face and found him looking right back at her. His hands were strong and tapered, the backs covered with tiny golden hairs—and oh, so sensual to watch.

Christi was matchmaking in the nicest possible way, doing nothing to force them together, but making sure they just spent time together. It was what Dizzy most needed, so that she could be sure of her feelings, and she silently thanked her friend for her tact.

It was a pleasant restaurant, cosy little tables in alcoves, subdued lighting; the sort of place for lovers to gaze across the table at each other and let their eyes talk of their love. The three of them looked a little out of place, a man alone with two young women.

'This will do wonders for your reputation, Uncle Zach,' Christi teased, seeming to pick up on her amused thoughts, not at all perturbed that neither of them had chosen to answer her earlier statement. '*Two* beautiful women!'

Zach smiled at her mischievous grin. 'I wasn't aware that my reputation needed ''wonders'' doing for it,' he drawled, very handsome in a dark brown suit that fitted him better than anything else Dizzy had seen him in, and a tie which was knotted meticulously at his throat. His hair had been neatly brushed back from his face when they met him in the entrance hall at the castle but, because it was still damp from his shower, and a light breeze blew outside, his hair now lay in an endearing wave across his forehead. She found everything about this man attractive, Dizzy admitted to herself in panic!

'Every man likes to have his ego boosted now and then,' Christi said with certainty.

'Taking my niece and her friend out to dinner doesn't do a thing for mine!' he returned drily.

Christi's friend—but that wasn't the only way he thought of her, Dizzy was sure of it. Tonight she was wearing the only other evening dress she carried around with her, a soft green dress that emphasised the colour of her eyes, making them look almost luminous. Zach's eyes, as he watched her descent down the stairs earlier, had told her that she was completely a woman to him, a woman he was very much aware of. Her hair had been loosely swept up on top of her head, giving her a sophistication that was usually lacking, and Zach had noticed that, too.

'Being escorted by a handsome man does a lot for mine,' Christi reproved. 'Doesn't it yours, Dizzy?'

She looked at Zach beneath lowered lashes, knowing by his embarrassed expression that he was uncomfortable with being called handsome, maybe even thought Christi was teasing him. And that would never do, not when he was the most attractive man in the room.

'Very much so,' she answered with firm sincerity, holding Zach's gaze. 'You underestimate yourself, Zach, if you think otherwise,' she told him softly.

Warmth blazed in his eyes, his gaze was deeply searching, and it was suddenly as if they were the only two people in the room, those lovers that Dizzy had imagined a few minutes ago, as they told of their feelings with their eyes. Zach's were saying he wanted her, and she was very much afraid hers were saying the same thing! And she still wasn't ready for this.

She looked away. 'It is very pleasant here,' she finally answered Christi's statement of a few minutes ago. 'Do you come here often, Zach?' she added politely, the smile on her lips distantly enquiring.

He shrugged, his gaze still intent. 'Never before, I'm afraid.'

'Uncle Zach doesn't have much of a social life usually, do you?' Christi said brightly.

Dizzy shot her friend a warning look, guessing she was trying to get Zach to admit to not being involved with anyone. She didn't know him that well, but the little she did know about him told her that he wouldn't have kissed her the way he had last night if there were another woman in his life.

'My work keeps me very busy,' he dismissed abruptly. 'I'm just a dull old professor of history, I'm afraid,' he added harshly.

'Dizzy doesn't find the subject boring at all,' Christi assured him enthusiastically. 'She has a passion for history; it was her favourite subject at school.'

Dizzy shot her a reproving look. 'I'm surprised you remember my favourite subject at school, we were never that—close,' she reminded drily.

Christi blushed as her enthusiasm for match-making overshadowed her good sense, and made her briefly forget the tale she had told before and after Dizzy's arrival in the Lake District. 'I remember *that*,' she defended awkwardly, 'because it was *my* worst subject!'

'Does anyone want any more coffee?' Dizzy affected a yawn. 'I'm a little tired after my disturbed night last night.' She deliberately kept her gaze averted from Zach, as she recalled all too vividly just how responsible he had been for the unsettling feelings.

'Mrs Scott told me that you sat with Kate for some time after I'd gone to bed,' Zach frowned.

She shrugged. 'I'd told her I would sit with her.'

'But she was asleep.'

Dizzy looked up at him. 'She could have woken up, and then she would have known I'd broken my promise to her.' In fact, she had sat with Kate until Mrs Scott began to stir at seven o'clock, only snatching a couple of hours' sleep before joining

Christi for a late breakfast, her friend having slept through the whole thing.

Zach was giving her a searching look, as if she puzzled him more than anything else he had ever experienced. 'You must be extremely tired,' he finally conceded softly, signalling for the bill.

Actually, she knew that, as with every other night, once she got to bed, no matter how tired she was, she wouldn't be able to sleep for hours yet. She had finished reading the two books she brought with her, as she had expected to be able to indulge herself in Zachariah Bennett's library. With that painting in there that was now impossible.

She accompanied Christi to the Ladies' room while Zach paid the bill, securing a couple of loose tendrils of hair while her friend renewed her make-up. Not that Christi needed the aid of much artifice, her features already perfect, her colour naturally attractive.

'You were doing very well until the end,' she finally told her friend drily.

Christi blushed. 'I was only trying to give the two of you a push in the right direction,' she said uncomfortably. 'Really, Dizzy, the man eats you up with his eyes and talks to you like a polite stranger!'

So Christi hadn't missed that burning look that had passed between them! 'It's only been three days, Christi,' she teased. 'I know patience isn't one of your virtues, but neither Zach or I are the type to leap into a relationship until we're ready for it.'

'You could have left to become a nun and he could have entered a monastery before either of you realise that you actually glow when you look at each other!' Christi said disgustedly.

Dizzy smiled. 'I have no inclination to become a nun,' she chuckled. 'And I don't think Zach has the qualifications to become a monk!'

'Really?' Christi pounced interestedly.

She blushed as she realised the trap she had fallen into. But any man who kissed like Zach did, who made her feel the way he did, couldn't possibly spend the rest of his life denying himself the 'pleasures of the flesh'. It would be a crime to himself and the vocation.

'Really,' she acknowledged drily. 'And that's all you're getting from me tonight, young lady,' she added firmly as Christi's eyes glowed with satisfaction.

'It's enough,' Christi said with glee. 'Believe me, it's enough!'

She smiled indulgently at Christi's buoyant mood as they went out to join her uncle. Even though it would spoil all Christi's plans if Dizzy and Zach did fall in love, her friend was pleased for her, not worrying about what she stood to lose. It was typical of Christi's generosity.

She watched Zach surreptitiously beneath lowered lashes on the drive back to the castle, Christi having announced, when they reached the car, that she intended 'stretching out' on the back seat, giving Dizzy no choice but to take the seat next to Zach.

With Christi sitting so quietly in the back it was almost possible to believe she and Zach were returning after a date together, that the evening would end in a lingering goodnight kiss once they reached the castle. She gave a disappointed sigh that it wasn't to be so, for she had a burning curiosity to be back in Zach's arms.

'That was a big sigh.' He turned to her briefly, smiling gently.

She glanced at Christi in the back. Her friend was giving a good impression of being asleep even if she wasn't, her eyes firmly closed as she leant back against the seat.

She turned back to Zach. 'I was thinking of last night,' she told him honestly, her voice low.

He frowned. 'Kate——'

'No—not Kate,' she said firmly.

Zach looked at her sharply, swerving the car suddenly as the movement of a rabbit in the road caught his eyes. He drew in a controlling breath after straightening the car, keeping his gaze firmly ahead. 'Not Kate?' he repeated with forced lightness.

'No,' she confirmed.

He breathed raggedly. 'Dizzy——'

'It's all right.' She put a hand on his arm. 'You don't have to say anything. They were my thoughts,' she dismissed with a shrug.

'And if mine have been the same all evening?' he bit out raspingly. 'Despite my assurances to you this morning?'

Her eyes were wide in the darkness. 'Zach?'

'Yes—Zach,' he echoed disgustedly. 'I'm too old to be having the thoughts I've been having about you! So much for my apology this morning——'

'Christi,' she reminded him softly, sure that her friend was no more asleep that she was, but she did have a ringside seat to a very personal conversation!

'Yes,' he conceded impatiently, his strong hands tightly gripping the wheel.

They lapsed into a silence that lasted until they reached the castle, Dizzy giving her friend a rueful smile as she made a show of supposedly waking up when the car came to a halt. She and Zach had been talking softly, and Christi may not have heard all of their conversation, but Dizzy didn't doubt she had heard enough!

Christi kept her expression bland as they all went into the lounge for the nightcap Zach had suggested; Dizzy couldn't get her to meet her gaze at all. And as Zach handed her the small brandy she had asked for she found out why!

'Not for me thanks, Uncle Zach,' Christi refused the nightcap. 'I think I'll just get straight up to bed. I'll see you both in the morning,' she added lightly before leaving the room.

Her friend had left so abruptly that she left an awkward silence behind her. Dizzy had felt brave enough in the darkness of the car on the drive home, but being left alone here in the lounge with Zach was a different matter altogether. It wasn't that she was a tease, never that, but she was sure neither of them had any idea where they went from here, and Christi's leaving them alone like this had just precipitated the moment of truth.

'I *have* been thinking about you, Dizzy.' Zach suddenly spoke, staring down into his glass of whisky. 'I haven't come to any conclusions, but—damn it!' He slammed his glass down, taking hers out of her unresisting fingers and placing it beside his own. 'I know I said this wouldn't happen again, but——' He didn't finish the sentence, his mouth forcefully claiming hers instead.

It was more, so much more than she even remembered, and her memories were already so vividly disturbing!

Her body curved instinctively against Zach's, her arms moving impulsively about his neck, her lips parting beneath his as he had taught her last night.

He was every inch the Greek god; demanding, possessive, claiming her response as his right.

And it was his. There was no denying it any longer; she wanted this man, in every way it was possible to want a man. She wanted him to love, to care for, to be made love to by. Morning might bring back the uncertainties but she didn't think so. She was in love with Zach, completely, irrevocably, and she knew he was the type of man who would never hurt her intentionally.

Her joyous realisation of her love, a love she had thought never to feel for any man, made her response all the more intense, deepening the kiss as she knew she wanted to belong to this man completely.

There was no gentleness in Zach tonight, only fierce demand, a need to show them both this was what they wanted, what they needed to make them sane again.

And then it all changed, his lips nibbling at hers, his teeth gently biting, the pleasure-pain sending quivers of delight through her whole body. She trembled uncontrollably as his tongue moved slowly around her parted lips before plunging deeply inside.

Her legs gave way beneath her, and the strength she had seen that first day, and which she knew the tailoring of the brown suit hid, enabled Zach to swing her up into his arms before carrying her over to the sofa.

He sat down with her still in his arms, their mouths still fused, tasting her, taking her, again and again.

Dizzy felt weak with longing, with a burning that she couldn't control, her arms about Zach's neck as she clung to him.

While his lips and teeth nibbled at her exposed throat, his hands caressed the length of her body. Dizzy's breathing was erratic as he lightly grazed the sides of her breasts, and she gasped as she felt the light caress of his thumb-tip, her nipple hard and pulsating.

Her breasts were always the one part of her body she felt self-conscious about, having developed them long before most of her friends, but as Zach deftly unzipped her dress to expose the uptilted peaks to his heated gaze she knew only pride that she had been able to put that glow of pleasure in his golden eyes.

He pulled the dress lower, freeing her completely, his hand trembling slightly as he cupped one upward sweep, gazing his fill of the pink-tipped loveliness. And then he wasn't content to just look; his gaze briefly met hers, finding no resistance there as he slowly lowered his mouth to her breast.

It was like an electric shock, tiny pinpricks of pleasure that made her arch up into him, wanting more, receiving it as he nibbled and sucked, nibbled and sucked.

Her head moved back of its own volition, and she was sent into a frenzy of longing as Zach laved first one nipple then the other, her whole body a throbbing ache that needed to be assuaged.

She fell back on to the sofa, taking Zach with her, welcoming his weight against her, their thighs melded together as they moved restlessly against each other, needing to——

'My God, what the hell am I doing?' Zach's groan of self-condemnation halted the madness. Dizzy looked up at him with unfocusing eyes as he pulled himself up off the sofa; his suit jacket was still on, but his shirt had been partly unbuttoned down his chest by her eager fingers, seconds earlier. His hair fell rakishly across his forehead, his mouth looked as swollen from their kisses as hers felt; he looked exactly what he was, a man who had drawn back on the brink of making love!

Dizzy sat up shakily, doing her best to straighten her dress. 'It's all right, Zach——'

'It is *not* all right.' He impatiently pushed her shaking hands aside, to pull up her dress and rezip it, pausing to look into her too-wide eyes, the swollen vulnerability of her lips. He straightened abruptly, drawing in a deep breath. 'I will not take advantage of a guest under my own roof!' he rasped.

Dizzy swayed uncertainly, her hair in disarray about her shoulders. 'I——'

'I won't!' Zach said again firmly, bending down to kiss her hard on the lips before striding out of the room.

What if the guest *wanted* to be taken advantage of?

CHAPTER EIGHT

Dizzy was still mulling over the problem the next day as Christi berated her for not confiding in her what had happened after she'd gone to bed the evening before.

She was in love with Zach, admitted it, accepted it *and* the pain she knew could come along with the acceptance. But Zach was determined not to repeat last night while she was still his guest and, short of moving out to a hotel, she didn't see how they were going to go on from here. And they had to move on, had to discover exactly how they felt about each other.

'—don't you think?'

She blinked, looking up at Christi as she realised her friend had asked her a question. 'What did you say?'

Christi looked ready to explode. 'Will you please get your mind on this conversation?' she snapped. 'It's very rude of you to be lost in thoughts of last night when you refuse to tell me *what* those thoughts are!'

She smiled at her friend's frustration with her preoccupation. 'Sorry,' she grimaced ruefully.

Christi gave a disgusted sigh. 'I was saying that I think it's a little unfair of you not to confide in me, when I was the one who made it possible for you to be alone with Uncle Zach last night.'

Her smile deepened; she was completely at ease with her emotions now, knowing they had been inevitable from the moment she had first gazed at her 'Greek god'. And she was convinced that Zach was nothing like her parents, that he would never let her down the way they had. Admitting to loving him made her feel vulnerable, but at the same time she had never felt so alive and happy in her life. Figuring out what to do about this love, now that she cherished it, was what filled her thoughts at the moment.

'Don't think we didn't appreciate it,' she teased her friend.

Christi perked up interestedly. 'How much?'

She shrugged. 'Your uncle and I haven't spoken at all today, so what do you think?'

Zach had kept to his usual routine of an early walk, early breakfast, working in his study until lunch time, a quick lunch in there, and then disappearing for the afternoon. It had given her no opportunity to see him, let alone attempt a private conversation with him.

'I think the two of you are just being stubborn,' Christi said disgustedly. 'You're so right for each other.'

Her eyes widened. 'We are?'

'Of course you are,' Christi nodded impatiently, pacing the room, the two of them having just had coffee in the lounge after a late lunch.

Perhaps they were, although from what Zach had been led to believe about her it probably wasn't as apparent to him. He probably thought he was having a nervous breakdown, being attracted to a drifter and a sponger, a woman who shared a man's bed just because he was 'lonely and had soulful brown eyes'!

He would have to be told the truth about that before things went any further, and that could make things awkward for all of them. Even if Zach were still attracted to her, she had no reason to suppose he would want to be involved with a twenty-one-year-old virgin with as many hang-ups as she had. No man welcomed complications like that into his life!

'Maybe,' she said non-committally. 'But don't go making any plans for calling him Zach,' she warned ruefully. 'Even supposing your uncle does admit to being attracted to me—*supposing* he does——' she repeated firmly at Christi's sceptical snort '—I would say one night in his bed is all he would be interested in with a drifter like me who shares anyone's bed for the night just for somewhere to stay.'

'We'll see about that!' Christi said indignantly. 'He'll answer to me if he dares... Oh, God, what a mess I've made of things!' she groaned.

'You weren't to know this would happen.' Dizzy shook her head. 'None of us were.'

Christi straightened determinedly. 'Well, I'm going to go and tell him the truth right now, and be damned with the consequences.'

'Let me tell him.'

Christi halted at the door, her expression uncertain. 'I should really be the one——'

'Let me,' Dizzy repeated softly. 'I—there are some other things to discuss, too,' she reminded gently. 'Like my relationship to the artist of

Knollsley Hall and the portrait in the library,' she explained flatly as Christi looked puzzled.

'None of that was your fault,' Christi defended instantly. 'We don't get to choose who our parents are.'

'No,' she conceded dully. 'And they usually don't get to choose us, either.'

'Most parents would be proud to have you as their daughter,' her friend said indignantly.

She gave a bitter laugh. 'My parents aren't like "most parents".'

'Oh, I know that,' Christi said fiercely. 'Sometimes I could——'

'Don't waste your energy being angry at them,' Dizzy advised softly. 'I wasted too many years doing that. It just makes you bitter and twisted, and in the end achieves nothing.'

'Maybe you're right,' Christi accepted with a sigh. 'But Uncle Zach isn't going to be concerned because your father is Martin Ellington-James, and your mother is Valerie Sherman,' she said with certainty.

Her mouth twisted. 'But does it make me more acceptable, looking at the way I am and the way I live, to admit that they're my parents, or is it easier for him to believe I'm just an old school acquaintance whose parents lost their money several years ago?' She gave a rueful smile.

'We both know that neither of those versions are true,' Christi defended. 'Besides, we all have a secret or two it's difficult to admit to.'

'Including Zach?' she said disbelievingly.

'Including him,' Christi nodded. 'And your secrets aren't so deep and dark that they should matter. Good gracious, you can't really believe he *wants* to go on thinking you're a sponging drifter!'

She shrugged. 'The daughter of Martin Ellington-James, MP, isn't going to be quite so easy to dismiss as penniless Dizzy James.'

'Uncle Zach isn't like that,' her friend said with certainty. 'And he does care for you, I'm sure of it.'

She was sure he felt something for her, too, otherwise he wouldn't have drawn back last night, no matter what code of ethics he had been brought up with. But he had loved his fiancée, been devastated when she died, and second best in the life of the man she loved just wouldn't be enough for her.

'We'll see.' She gave Christi a reassuring smile.

'When?'

She blinked at the abruptness of Christi's question. 'When what?'

'When are you going to tell him?' her friend prompted determinedly.

'Well—I—the next time I see him, I suppose,' she shrugged.

'Why not now?' Christi pressured. 'He can't have gone far.'

If only Christi knew! Zach hadn't gone very far at all. But offering her the temptation of going in search of Zach, when she knew he was off bathing nude in a lake only two miles from here, was something she wasn't sure she could resist any longer. Maybe finding him at a disadvantage like that wouldn't make her feel quite so nervous about what she had to tell him.

'Go on,' Christi urged as she saw her hesitation. 'He always goes off towards the lakes,' she supplied eagerly. 'I suppose there are more birds to watch around there,' she shrugged.

Poor Christi didn't know her uncle at all if she still believed that bird-watching tale, although, if *she* hadn't seen Zach's nude bathing for herself that first day, perhaps she would have found it difficult to believe, too!

'OK.' She firmly made her decision. 'But if I'm not with him when he comes back send out a search party,' she attempted to tease.

Christi hugged her impulsively. 'Good luck.'

Dizzy gave a rueful smile. 'Just don't expect too much, hmm?'

'Are you kidding?' her friend grinned. 'I already have my bridesmaid's dress of sackcloth and ashes all picked out! Uncle Zach's sure to make me do some sort of penance for the lies I've told him about you,' she grimaced.

'Half-truths,' Dizzy comforted.

'Lies,' Christi insisted. 'Although maybe he'll be so relieved to know the truth he'll forget all about being angry with me,' she added hopefully.

Dizzy felt the same way herself. She had been a party to Christi's deception, even if she hadn't altogether approved of the idea.

She didn't exactly rush to the lake, for she was in no hurry to make her confessions.

She looked much as she had that first day, her hair confined in the thick braid down her spine, although, as usual, curling wisps insisted on framing her face. The baggy T-shirt was clean, even if it did nothing for her figure, the same with the faded and patched denims. She wasn't exactly dressed in a way guaranteed to convince Zach she was the daughter of very wealthy parents!

She could hear the splash of the water even before she came down the last hill that sided the lake, although it took her a few minutes to spot Zach's sleek head as he swam effortlessly about a hundred yards from the shore.

When he spotted her, was he going to walk unconcernedly out of the water, unselfconscious of his nakedness, or would he stay in the water that must still be a little chill, despite the warmth of summer?

She tensed nervously as she realised she was about to find out. Zach's gaze narrowed on her as he swam lazily back to the shore, where his clothes lay in a neat pile at her feet. After the intimacies they had shared the night before, she was self-conscious about facing him again, all the more so because she knew he was naked beneath the water.

She was unprepared for his opening comment as he trod water several feet away from her!

'I wondered if you would ever come back here.' He met her gaze steadily.

Dizzy gave a start of surprise, swallowing hard. 'Back?' she repeated in a voice that sounded slightly higher than normal.

He shrugged broad shoulders. 'From the time you must have arrived the other day, and the way you looked at me when we met, I suspected you might have seen me here on your way to the castle.'

Deep colour brightened her cheeks, and she thrust her hands into her denims pockets. 'Was it so obvious I was attracted to you?' she snapped.

'Hardly,' he drawled lightly. 'You looked more surprised than anything. But when you began to choke, as soon as Christi mentioned I had been bird-watching all afternoon, I was certain you must have seen what I was really doing.' He became suddenly still. 'Did you like what you saw, Dizzy?' he prompted huskily.

'I—yes,' she answered in a rush. 'I—I liked it very much.' Her cheeks felt as if they were on fire, her wide-eyed gaze fixed on him as she wondered if he intended walking out of the water to dry in the sun today.

Her eyes widened even more as he began to walk towards her, her breath catching in her throat, only to be released in an unsteady groan as black swimming trunks were revealed as he left the water behind him.

He shot her an amused glance as he picked up the towel from beneath his clothes, to begin drying his hair. 'What did you expect, Dizzy?' he teased softly. 'I haven't swum in the nude since I realised you must have seen me that day, and that you could do so again any time you felt like taking a walk down here.' He took pity on her, and explained, 'I've been waiting for some comment from Christi about my afternoon activities,' he added with a questioning look.

Dizzy shrugged, still slightly shaken by the expectancy she had felt as Zach waded out of the water towards her. Not that he was any less devastating in this minute pair of bathing trunks, with water glistening on the golden beauty of his body, and his true masculine power revealed.

'I didn't think it was right to tell Christi,' she sighed. 'It would have been almost like breaking a confidence.' Besides, it would have put her in the awkward position of trying to pretend Zach's nakedness that day had meant nothing to her!

He hung the towel around his neck, the impact of his honey-coloured eyes all the more apparent without his glasses, his hair falling untidily across his forehead. 'I'm glad you didn't say you didn't think Christi would be interested,' he drawled.

'Zach——'

'Dizzy,' he derided.

She frowned. He seemed different today somehow, almost as if—as if he were *flirting* with her! And why shouldn't he? After last night he must think she was more than willing to fall into his arms any time he asked her to.

Zach watched her curiously. 'What's Christi up to, Dizzy?' he finally asked. 'And why have you let her get away with it?'

She blinked, dragging her gaze away from the flatness of his chest and stomach, and up to meet his golden gaze. She instantly felt as if she were drowning in a sea of sensuous honey.

'Dizzy.' He took the step that separated them, clasping her arms. 'I've known from the first time I kissed you that your experience with men must have been limited to the platonic rather than the sensual,' he told her gently.

She shook her head. 'How could you know that?' she defended. 'I haven't——'

'I know because of this, Dizzy.' Even as he spoke huskily, his head was lowering to hers, his thumb on her chin, parting her lips to receive his, gently savouring the taste of her before deepening the kiss.

Her hands were drawn instinctively to touch him, to feel the silky texture of his skin, to know the strength of the muscles that rippled beneath that skin. He was steel and velvet at the same time, and her fingertips tingled as she touched him, her hands moving up and down the strength of his back, halting uncertainly as she encountered the material of his bathing trunks.

His lips left hers to travel across her cheek. 'Yes,' he encouraged gruffly. 'Touch me, Dizzy!' he urged at her self-conscious hesitation.

He was like satin to touch, a flesh sculpture, perfect in every way. And from the reaction of his body, her inexperienced caresses pleased him immensely.

Finally he put her away from him, gazing down at her with warm eyes. 'We have to talk,' he said apologetically.

Dizzy's senses were so fevered that it took her a few moments to realise he didn't intend making love to her. 'But we aren't in your home now,' she pointed out disappointedly.

He smiled gently. 'We're still on my land. And we have several things to talk out before we do anything else. Shall we make ourselves comfortable first?' he suggested softly.

She was very much afraid that making themselves 'comfortable' included Zach putting his clothes on, and as Zach began to do just that she bit back her regretful sigh and sat down on the grass to wait for him to join her.

Dressed in the professor's clothes, his hair neatly brushed, he made it seem as if the moment of closeness a few minutes earlier had not happened.

Zach carefully filled and lit his pipe before joining her on the grass, sitting a polite distance away, as if he, too, felt the chasm yawning between them.

'Tell me,' he leant back against a tree, the smoke from his pipe filling the air, 'who is Henry?'

It had been the last question she had expected, and for a few seconds she just stared at him. 'Henry?' she finally managed to repeat.

'Yes,' he nodded. 'Whoever he was, he certainly wasn't your lover,' he added with certainty.

'Did I ever say he was?' she defended indignantly.

'Stop delaying the inevitable, Dizzy,' he said wearily, the glasses back as a screen between her and his emotions. 'Is Henry a boyfriend of Christi's she doesn't want me to know about?'

'Certainly not,' she frowned.

Zach sighed. 'Well, my dear niece is definitely hiding something.'

Dizzy blushed. 'Then why don't you ask her these questions?' She pulled up a blade of grass beside her, ripping it to shreds in her agitation.

He watched her steadily. 'Because you're as involved in this as she is,' he stated calmly. 'The two of you are so familiar and at ease with each other that it speaks of a long and loyal friendship, not the old school acquaintances who can barely stand each other, but feel a certain loyalty because of a girlish equivalent of the "old school tie", that you would have me believe.'

She had *told* Christi that wouldn't work, knew they had given themselves away numerous times

over the last few days. And Zach was far from the
unobservant man buried in his books that Christi
seemed to believe him to be!

'If you weren't so judgemental, Christi wouldn't
have had to try to convince you of her maturity to
handle her own money by showing you just how
irresponsible she could be but isn't!' Dizzy attacked, breathing hard in her anger. Zach had lulled
her into a false sense of security with his kisses and
caresses, leaving her defences wide open, she realised now, when it was too late to do anything
about them. Christi knew she was going to tell Zach
the truth, but she doubted her friend expected it to
be in quite this way, she thought in dismay!

Zach's eyes narrowed behind the glasses. 'Is that
what the two of you have been doing?'

She shrugged resentfully. 'Well, you have to admit
that I'm a perfect example of irresponsibility!'

'Not quite,' he drawled, his gaze considering.
'Who are you?'

Her head went back. 'Dizzy James.'

'Who are you really?' he repeated in a hard voice.

She drew in a ragged breath. 'A friend of
Christi's.'

'That's obvious,' he bit out raspingly. 'But it
doesn't answer my question.'

He was angry, angrier than her, and she couldn't
really blame him after the stupid, *stupid* game she
and Christi had been playing at his expense.

She swallowed hard. 'If I tell you my father's
name is—is Martin Ellington-James,' she completed almost defiantly at his compelling glance,
'maybe that will help you,' she snapped.

Zach gave a puzzled frown. 'I didn't know he had remarried.'

'He hasn't,' she scorned. 'And no, I'm not illegitimate, either,' she derided at the surprised rise of his eyebrows, her mouth twisting mockingly as she saw the truth dawn in those expressive eyes.

'Your mother is Valerie Sherman?' He spoke slowly, as if still uncertain of his facts.

'That's right, Professor.' As usual, she was on the defensive when discussing either of her parents, the shield over her emotions, which she had allowed to slip while she searched her feelings for this man, firmly back in place. She had been a fool to believe they could ever care for each other!

'Then Knollsley Hall was your home?' he enunciated carefully, as if he still couldn't believe what he was being told.

Knollsley Hall hadn't been her home, it had been her prison! Oh, until her mother had left when she was four it had had the semblance of a home, but after that it had become somewhere to escape from. But very few people knew or understood that, and she wasn't about to confide in Zach, now that they were suddenly so distant from each other. She should have known better than to allow her emotions to take over, even briefly!

'It was my father's home.' She gave a cool inclination of her head.

'Then you went to live with your mother after the divorce?' Zach sounded puzzled.

Dizzy gave an impatient sigh. 'I don't think where I spent my childhood has any relevance to this conversation,' she bit out dismissively.

'Now that we've established that, far from having fallen on ill-fortune, and so leaving you to make your way in the world as best you can, your father is one of the richest MPs in the country—and that's saying a lot!—and your mother is a very wealthy artist,' Zach acknowledged disgustedly, 'I don't think your privileged background has any more relevance to the conversation, either!' he bit out grimly.

Privileged background! Was it privileged to be ignored by her father until she was four and her mother ran away from him, when she then became the only thing he could vent his anger and frustration on without fear of retribution? Was it privileged when she was sent away to school at eight so that he didn't have to see her marked resemblance to her mother as she got older? Was it privileged when he wouldn't even have her back in the house for the holidays after that first year, because each time he saw her she reminded him of the woman who had walked out on both of them, so that she either had to remain at the school during holiday times or accept the open invitation she always had from Christi's parents to stay with them? If that was privilege then she didn't know what abuse was!

Tears glistened in her pained green eyes, tears she quickly blinked away as she met Zach's gaze steadily. 'I'm twenty-one now, my parents are no longer responsible for me, and as you can see I live my life the way I want to,' she told him defiantly. 'Who my parents are doesn't change the fact that I live out of a backpack, stay with friends whenever I can. Whereas Christi——'

'Christi has some explaining of her own to do,' Zach cut in harshly, standing up. 'Now that I know the truth, your presence here is no longer necessary, to give a false impression, or try to convince a rather staid professor of history that he's the best thing you've seen since sliced bread——'

'I *hate* sliced bread,' Dizzy put in defensively. 'And all of my responses to you have been real!'

His mouth twisted as he looked down at her. 'A sham,' he corrected bitterly. 'But you have no further need to sacrifice yourself in the name of friendship——'

'It was no sacrifice!' Dizzy derided.

His mouth firmed angrily. 'I'm sure Henry is just longing for you to return to his bed. Possibly he finds your act of innocence more to his liking than I did!'

They were hitting out at each other in angry defiance, each blow more cutting than the last, until in the end they would rip each other apart. Zach believed she was responsible for playing with his emotions because she was trying to help Christi, and he wasn't about to forgive her for that.

Looking at this from his point of view, what choice did he have? She had lied to him; why shouldn't he think her innocence was all a lie, too?

'Possibly,' she said heavily, standing up to brush the grass from her hands and denims. 'I take it you want me to move out of the castle as soon as possible?' All her anger had gone now, leaving her aching inside like never before.

'If not sooner,' Zach confirmed harshly.

She drew in a ragged breath. 'I'll make sure you don't have to see me again before I leave.'

He nodded abruptly. 'I would appreciate that,' he bit out.

Dizzy bowed her head. 'I thought you might.'

'Now I have to go and find your partner in crime,' he said grimly, a steely quality in his voice that she had never heard before. 'But I'd like you to know you could have both saved yourselves all this trouble.'

Dizzy looked up at him dazedly. What did he mean by that?

He gave a bitter smile. 'I invited Christi up here so that we could get to know each other a little better, perhaps cement a friendship, before I released my guardianship of her and we perhaps drifted apart. Which would have been a pity when we're the only family each of us have.' He returned Dizzy's stunned gaze contemptuously. 'I never had any intention of not releasing Christi's inheritance once she's twenty-one!'

CHAPTER NINE

'COULD you put your hand a little to the left of Jim's chest, please, Heather?' Dizzy instructed distractedly, gazing in dissatisfaction at the couple across the room. 'That's perfect,' she nodded, as the other woman complied.

A bitter smile curved Dizzy's lips as she wondered what interpretation Zach would put on this situation if he were to walk in now.

Not that there was much chance of that. She had been back in London since yesterday, and she hadn't heard a word from Zach *or* Christi.

Christi and Zach had already been in his study by the time she had followed him back to the castle, and so she had quietly packed her bags and left, knowing that Christi was in enough trouble without her adding to it by hanging around when she had bluntly been told to leave. She had no doubt that Christi would contact her once she got back to London herself.

But it hadn't made the waiting any easier, and, after a night of lying awake thinking of Zach and the misunderstandings between them, she had decided that indulging in her other love in life was what she needed to take her mind off him. Heather and Jim had been only too pleased to come over when she called them.

Her father had never considered the artistic talent that she had inherited from her mother to be a

foundation for a career, but had called the accurate
drawings she would present to him as a child's
'scribblings', until in the end she stopped sharing
them with him.

The boarding-school had been even less thrilled
by her talent, more interested in the academic than
the arts. The teachers had not been at all impressed
with the caricatures she often did of them to amuse
her classmates, and more than once her drawing
equipment had been confiscated.

But her talent for sketching and painting had
been the one thing she *was* grateful to accept from
her mother, and she knew by the time she was
eighteen that, whatever career she chose, it had to
involve sketching of some kind. With her mother
already established as an accomplished artist, it had
narrowed her field down somewhat unless she
wanted to be constantly referred to as 'Valerie
Sherman's daughter'. As that was the last thing she
had ever wanted to be known as, she had steered
very clear of that area of art.

Once again, it had been Christi who set her on
the right track, introducing her to a family friend
who also happened to own a publishing house, and
who was always on the look-out for illustrators for
the covers of his books. With her avid interest in
history, and her artistic talent, Dizzy had been a
natural at producing the glossy evocative covers that
enticed a reader to pick up a book to read the back
cover and see what the story was about.

Her year of working for Astro Publishing had
been an experience she would always be grateful
for, bringing her worldwide recognition for the DC
James illustrations that firmly established her at the

top of her field. The last two years on her own had been filled with hundreds of offers of work, both here and in North America, and she hadn't refused any of them that looked interesting, enjoying the travelling almost as much as she did the work. There was just one professional dream she had left to fulfil, a dream that didn't seem to stand much chance of becoming reality when Claudia Laurence, the one author she longed to illustrate for, didn't seem to have heard of her *or* the provocative covers she had given to dozens of historical romances!

Her studio, and the place where she occasionally stayed for a few days between assignments, was at the top of an old warehouse that had later been converted to flats: a huge barn of a place that gave her the space and light she needed to work. It couldn't exactly be called her home, but it was the closest she came to calling anywhere that.

She was working on a Regency cover right now, Heather wearing a delicate pink dress that was cut in the alarmingly low fashion of the day, Jim every inch the aristocratic duke as he looked down his haughty nose at the saucy young woman of spirit he would eventually marry. For some illustrators this could just have been another one of 'those' covers, but each piece of work Dizzy produced was special to her, and to the people who constantly wrote, praising her work. She never ceased to be thrilled herself when she knew she had done a good job.

Unfortunately, today wasn't going to be one of those days! Try as she might to put all thought of Zach out of her mind, seeing how close the couple were she was supposed to be photographing only

reminded her that hours ago *she* had been in Zach's
arms. That was before everything had all blown up
in her face.

If Christi didn't call her soon and tell her what
was going on she was going to wring her friend's
neck when she *did* see her again!

Christi had to know how worried she was. Or
perhaps her friend was so devastated by the obvious retribution her uncle could give for her
scheme that she didn't feel like talking to anyone
just now!

Zach *had* been very angry yesterday, everything
Dizzy had told him seeming only to convince him
she had gone further than trying to help convince
him of Christi's maturity, that she had tried to use
a relationship between the two of *them* to try and
persuade him to release Christi's money.

Money had never been important to her on an
everyday basis; as long as she had enough to live
on, she wasn't interested in 'putting money aside
for a rainy day'. Life was too short and precarious
for that. But she had been lucky, she was paid well
for doing something that she loved, and so, despite
all her feelings to the contrary, she had managed
to amass a small fortune. Her father would be
stunned if he knew how much his daughter was
worth! She had decided from the first not to confide
in him about her career, had deliberately chosen to
illustrate under the name DC James because of that.
No doubt knowing that she earned her living legit-
imately, after all, would give him a certain amount
of relief, but knowing what that work was was sure
to bring down his scorn on her. He had been scandalised that his wife could choose to be an artist,

so God knew what he would make of the provocatively lovely covers she chose to illustrate to whet people's appetite for the story between those covers! She certainly wasn't in any hurry to find out!

Possibly Zach would view it the same way; it certainly wasn't the type of thing a professor of history would like the woman in his life to be involved in!

Not that she *was* the woman in his life. They may have come close—Zach's gentle lovemaking before he learnt the truth about her and Christi had certainly given her hope—but she had watched as that was slowly destroyed with each new thing she revealed about herself. Far from believing in the innocence he had guessed at as he made love to her, he now believed she was a better actress than Christi could ever be!

'Dizzy, are you all right?'

She looked up at the couple across the room as Heather spoke concernedly, realising as she did so that she had been staring fixedly at the floor for the last five minutes. She gave a rueful smile, realising that the photographs she had intended taking, so that she could later do her preliminary sketching from them, weren't even half done.

She straightened. 'I'm afraid I'm not really in the mood for this today,' she said apologetically. 'Do you mind if we stop now?'

'Not at all,' Jim replied for both of them. The couple instantly relaxed their pose, both he and Heather were actors who modelled when they weren't doing other work. 'Are you sure you're feeling all right? You don't seem like yourself today.'

If only she *were* someone else! If only she could have listened to Zach's accusations and then neatly turned around and told him she hadn't been in his arms for any other reason than that she loved him. But love was too new to her, the feeling of vulnerability leaving her too raw to pain, for her to do anything else but back away from it. She was very much afraid she had had her one chance at love, and lost it.

'I don't think my short holiday did me any good.' She gave a forced smile. 'Could you both come back tomorrow?' she said hopefully, very much aware that time was passing and that she had done little or nothing towards this cover.

'Morning?' Heather suggested with a frown. 'I have a cover to do for Carla in the afternoon.'

Carla Fortune was an illustrator who worked mainly on mysteries, but both Heather and Jim were very much in demand by most illustrators, both of them having that elusive quality that allowed them to express the exact emotions required. It didn't surprise Dizzy in the least that she was going to have to wait in line for them, in fact, she had been thrilled earlier when they had been able to come over for a few hours this morning. Probably Carla had Heather booked for this afternoon, too!

'That's fine,' she nodded. 'I——' She broke off as the doorbell rang, her heart starting to pound as she hoped it was Christi. 'Why don't the two of you get changed while I answer the door?' she suggested nervously. 'I—you—I'll see you both tomorrow,' she added in a rush, before hurrying to the door.

Christi looked just the same as she usually did, beautiful and calm, striding past Dizzy into the studio, turning back to her chidingly after taking in the photographic equipment.

'I should have known you would get straight back to work,' she drawled, throwing off the linen jacket, that matched the blue sheath of a dress she wore, before dropping down tiredly on to one of the over-stuffed cushions that served as Dizzy's chairs. 'I feel as if I haven't stopped running the last twenty-four hours.' She rested massaging fingertips against her aching temples.

Dizzy swallowed nervously, standing across the room from her friend. 'From your uncle?' she prompted, in a voice too casual to be genuine.

Christi looked up at her with accusing eyes. 'Well, didn't *you*?'

She sighed, moving to switch off the bright lights that had spotlighted Heather and Jim minutes earlier. 'He told me to go,' she muttered.

'Well, of course he told you to go,' Christi said disgustedly. 'You gave him the impression you were some sort of trap we both wanted him to walk into, so that it made it easier asking him to release my money!'

Dizzy turned sharply, her eyes blazing. 'I did no such thing!' she snapped fiercely. 'That was the conclusion that he *enjoyed* jumping to,' she scorned hardily.

'And that you were too proud to refute,' Christi rebuked.

'That I didn't get the *chance* to refute,' she corrected firmly, her hands clenched at her sides. 'He wasn't prepared to listen to anything I had to say

once he knew my parents were Martin Ellington-
James and Valerie Sherman. He seemed to find my
"privileged" background totally suited to the
teasing little vamp who tried to make a fool out of
him!'

'Oh, Dizzy,' Christi groaned apologetically.

'For God's sake, don't pity me,' she warned
fiercely, holding on to her emotions with tremen-
dous effort. 'I'll fall apart into a million pieces if
you do that!' she explained shakily.

Christi flinched, her eyes pained. 'You're in love
with him.'

It wasn't a question, just a statement of fact, a
fact that had to be all too obvious to this woman
who knew her so well. 'A lot of good it's done me,'
she dismissed brittly. 'I always said love was a very
overrated emotion.' She tried to sound lightly un-
concerned, but unfortunately her voice broke
emotionally, and she only sounded as devastated as
she was.

'Oh, love, it isn't——' Christi broke off awkwardly as Heather and Jim came out of the room
they had been using to change in. 'Hi,' she greeted
brightly to cover Dizzy's obvious distress if anyone
looked at her too closely. 'What were you today,
Jim?' she said familiarly. 'A reformed outlaw or a
rampaging Viking?'

He grinned, straightening his jacket. 'A cynical
duke,' he drawled.

'Oh, one of those!' Christi nodded ruefully. 'In
that case, you must have been the Simpering Miss,
Heather,' she teased lightly.

Heather shook down her long red hair, obviously relieved to have it loose about her shoulders

once more. 'None of Dizzy's heroines ever look *simpering*,' she said, scandalised, her eyes glowing with laughter. 'Even though the hero and heroine have all their clothes on—usually—Dizzy still manages to imply the sensuality boiling beneath the surface.'

'You've got the job, Heather.' Dizzy was in control again now, at least, on the surface. 'No need to overdo it,' she chided self-derisively.

Their laughter served to ease the awkwardness when Jim and Heather had come into the room, the other couple taking their leave a few minutes later.

'Just tell me,' Dizzy turned back to Christi once they were alone, 'did Zach get really angry and tell you you would have to wait for your money, or did he keep to his initial decision to let you have it when you're twenty-one?' She held her breath as she waited for the answer, knowing there was no chance of Zach ever forgiving her for her part in this if he had decided to make Christi wait until she was twenty-five.

'He *was* angry, wasn't he?' Christi grimaced expressively. 'When he came back to the castle after talking to you, I thought he was going to——'

'Christi!'

'Sorry,' her friend sighed at her unmistakable tension. 'Well, he——' She broke off as the telephone began to ring.

Dizzy scowled at the interruption. 'It's like Picccadilly Circus in here this morning!' She glared, grabbing the receiver and barking a response into the mouth-piece.

Whatever she had been expecting—if she had been expecting anything—it wasn't what her friend and agent, Dick Crosby, was telling her!

'Claudia Laurence has asked for you to do her next cover,' Dick announced triumphantly.

Was this the way it worked: fate took away one dream and replaced it with another? She had lost Zach, but she could have the Claudia Laurence cover instead? Given a free choice, there was no way she would have chosen to have it that way around.

'Dizzy, I said you've got it.' Dick sounded puzzled at her silence. 'The new Claudia Laurence cover is yours!'

She had heard him the first time, and she had thought that if this day ever came it would be the happiest time of her life, illustrating for her favourite author having been what she had always considered the pinnacle of her career. Now it didn't seem important at all, nothing did.

'Dizzy——'

She heard no more as the receiver was gently taken out of her hand and Christi took control of her end of the conversation, after identifying herself.

However, Christi seemed as stunned by the news as Dizzy was! 'What did you say?' she demanded sharply, her hand tightly gripping the receiver. 'Sorry,' she muttered as Dick obviously made it clear he didn't welcome that sort of reaction from her, too! 'They did? She did?' Her eyes lit up excitedly as Dick related the details.

Dizzy turned away. This was what she had always wanted, what she had dreamt of, but loving Zach, losing him, had taken away her pleasure in anything, even something that had once been as important to her as this.

Was this what her life was going to be like from now on, this flat, nothingness existence, where nothing really mattered any more? How could she stand it? She didn't have any other choice *but* to stand it, unless she went to Zach and begged him to listen to her, to believe her.

Was she really that desperate? Yes, she was! Could she do something like that? Not yet, she recognised sadly. Maybe in a few days, when the initial heartache had eased to a dull throb instead of this tearing ache inside her, maybe then she would be able to accept it if Zach still rejected her, even after she had convinced him she really did love him.

While she had been asking herself questions, and then answering them, Christi had been involved in an excited conversation with Dick. 'She'll be there,' she concluded firmly before ringing off.

Dizzy frowned. 'I take it that was me you were talking about?' she derided wryly.

'It most certainly was,' Christi nodded, her air of suppressed excitement unmistakable.

'And just where will I be?' she mocked drily.

'Empire Publishing,' her friend supplied economically. 'This afternoon. Two o'clock.'

'Don't you think you should have consulted me before—— This afternoon?' she echoed disbelievingly. 'At *two* o'clock?' she repeated, with even more disbelief. 'But that's only just over an hour away,' she protested after glancing at the wall-clock.

Christi nodded. 'Which is why you have to get ready and go now. You can't wear jeans, of course, so——'

'Christi, I'm not in the mood to go and see a publisher this afternoon!' she groaned emotionally.

'Not the publisher.' Christi had already walked through to Dizzy's bedroom and was sorting through the meagre contents of her wardrobe, obviously finding nothing there that suited her. 'Although I suppose he'll be there,' she dismissed vaguely, holding up a green suit against Dizzy for inspection, then shaking her head with a horrified groan, both of them recognising the suit as the one Dizzy had left school in three years earlier. 'You're going to meet the author herself, Dizzy.' She resumed looking in the wardrobe, sighing as the only thing left that she hadn't already rejected was a pale green sun-dress that wasn't really suitable for visiting a publisher and his famous author in either. 'It will have to do, I suppose.' She pulled it out resignedly. 'It probably makes you look about sixteen, but . . .' She didn't need to finish the sentence, her disgust was obvious. 'I'd lend you this dress and jacket, but it would probably reach down to your ankles——'

'Besides having to be split in the bodice to accommodate another part of my anatomy,' Dizzy drawled.

'Hmm.' Christi looked at the part of Dizzy's anatomy in question as she obediently buttoned on the sun-dress after stripping off her denims and T-shirt. 'Maybe you don't look sixteen, after all!' she admired, as the dress left no doubt as to the full curve of Dizzy's breasts.

'Christi.' She halted her friend in the act of un-plaiting her hair so that she could brush it loose about her shoulders. 'Much as I appreciate your help,' she mocked lightly, 'I'm really not in the mood to see an author this afternoon, either.'

'It's not just "an author", Dizzy,' her friend re-proved in a shocked voice. 'It's Claudia Laurence!'

She sighed. 'I'm not in the mood to meet her, either.'

Christi stared at her as if she had gone insane, giving a sudden shake of her head. 'Of course you are,' she decided briskly. 'Do you have any sandals to go with this dress——'

'Christi, I really don't want to go,' she said wearily.

'Well, you're going,' her friend decided stub-bornly. 'Claudia Laurence asked for you personally.'

'And it's very nice,' Dizzy nodded. 'But not this afternoon, hmm?'

'Most definitely this afternoon,' Christi told her firmly. 'Apparently, your Miss Laurence is some-thing of a recluse, and she's only up to town this afternoon before going back to her home.'

'I never knew that,' Dizzy frowned. 'I knew she didn't like publicity, but I never realised she ac-tively avoided it.'

'According to Dick, you're very privileged,' her friend confirmed. 'Oh, come on, Dizzy,' she en-couraged as she still hesitated. 'You're not doing any good just sitting around here, moping!'

Was that was she was doing? Yes, it was. She was also asking herself a lot of questions she didn't like the answers to!

'All right.' She gave in with a deep sigh. 'And the sandals are at the back of the wardrobe,' she added in answer to Christi's earlier question to avoid having Christi tell her she was doing the right thing by getting on with her life. She knew she was doing the right thing, but that didn't make it any easier!

Christi looked down at the darkness at the bottom of the cupboard, pulling out the pair of black sandals that stood next to a pair of disreputable sneakers. 'I'm not surprised I missed seeing them among all your other shoes,' she derided disgustedly.

Dizzy couldn't help laughing at her friend's horrified expression; Christi possessed suitable shoes, in almost every available colour there was. It felt good to laugh, even if it was about something as silly as her own lack of shoes. What did she need dozens of pairs of shoes for? She could only wear one pair at a time!

Christi didn't quite seem to have forgiven her as she accompanied her in the taxi to Empire Publishing, although she was somewhat mollified by the fact that Dizzy had let her loosen her hair after all. Not that she thought David Kendrick would be that impressed by her appearance; the previous half-dozen times she had met the dynamic young publisher she had been wearing her customary jeans and T-shirt! However, she didn't tell Christi that; in her place, her friend would have lost no opportunity to try and romantically interest the multi-millionaire, and would be horrified that Dizzy had so blatantly thrown away the chance. She hadn't seen it that way herself at the time, but had merely seen it as being herself.

But owning up to being herself didn't seem to have got her very far with the man she *did* love, so she doubted this transformation would interest David in the least, either. Still, it had kept Christi happy, and as her friend was having to come back to the studio this evening, so that they could finish their earlier conversation, that wasn't a bad thing. An uncooperative Christi could be very uncomfortable indeed.

'I'll come back to the studio about eight,' Christi confirmed as she stayed in the taxi after Dizzy had got out at the Empire Publishing building. 'Good luck,' she called out as Dizzy entered the building.

She turned to give her a vaguely reassuring smile, giving herself a pep-talk as she was shown up to David's office. This was the opportunity she had been waiting for, she mustn't ruin it all now just because her heart was breaking. *Just* because? Good God, she had never known such unbearable pain before.

'Go right in,' David's secretary told her smilingly as soon as she entered the outer office. 'He's expecting you.'

Empire Publishing had been started by David only ten years ago, but in that time it had grown to challenge all the more established publishing houses, mainly, Dizzy knew, because of the unshakable enthusiasm and instincts of its creator, David Kendrick. He was that unusual thing today, a youthful entrepreneur who seemed to make a success of everything he did. And he fired those around him with the same enthusiasm. Dizzy wasn't at all surprised when Claudia Laurence had begun to be published by him five years ago, the partnership launching both parties into the higher echelon of their professions.

This was her own opportunity to be touched by their magic and, for this brief time at least, she had to put Zach out of her mind.

Which wasn't all that easy to do, when the first person she saw as she opened the office door was Zachariah Bennett, standing in front of the window, the sunshine turning his hair to gold!

She blinked, sure that when she opened her eyes it would be David standing there, dark-haired David with the deep blue eyes, not the golden-haired Greek god who haunted her every moment.

Zach was still standing there when she opened her eyes, the same Zach who made her body quiver and her heart beat erratically, and yet not the same Zach at all. Gone was the absent-minded professor with his ill-fitting clothes and endearing ways, and in his place was a man who wore the expensively tailored brown suit and cream shirt with an elegance that left no doubt as to his virility. His hair was shorter, too, and had been styled so that it fell enchantingly across his forehead, drawing attention to the golden eyes that she had always guessed had no necessity of the heavy-rimmed glasses he had so easily discarded today.

She wasn't sure she was at all comfortable with this new Zach!

But what was he doing here at all? She had come here to see David Kendrick, this was his office, and yet she and Zach were alone. She didn't understand this at all. And there was nothing to be gained from looking at Zach, for his expression was enigmatic in the extreme.

She shifted uncomfortably. 'I think there must have been some sort of mistake——'

'No mistake, Dizzy,' he spoke huskily, crossing the room to close the door behind her, stepping back to look down at her.

There was complete silence in the room, and the office was so high up the building that all Dizzy could see out of the window was sky; it was as if she and Zach were suddenly completely alone in the world, not a sound penetrating the room.

'I came to see David Kendrick,' she began awkwardly, wondering if, somewhere between getting out of the taxi downstairs and arriving up here, she could have gone insane. What other explanation could there be for Zach being in David Kendrick's office?

'He told me you were coming to see Claudia Laurence.' Zach gazed down at her intently.

Dizzy avoided direct contact with that glance, knowing she *would* go insane if she should actually lose herself in that honey-brown. 'What are *you* doing here, Zach?' she asked flatly.

'I wanted to talk to you——'

Her eyes blazed as she looked up at him. 'Wouldn't it have been easier coming to my studio— which I'm sure Christi must have told you about— than setting up this elaborate charade?' She drew in a steadying breath as her voice rose emotionally. 'Isn't it enough that I know how contemptuous you are of me?' she spoke levelly. 'Are you so angry about what Christi and I did to you that you want to discredit me in the only world I'm comfortable in?' She looked at him with pained disbelief.

The fact that there was no Claudia Laurence cover after all didn't bother her, but that Zach disliked her enough to go to this extreme did!

'David Kendrick is a friend of mine,' Zach told her gently. 'This "charade", as you call it, will go no further than this room. And I'm not angry with you, Dizzy. I'm not sure anger was ever the way to describe how I felt when you told me the truth about yourself yesterday,' he added heavily.

'Then maybe it was what Christi told you about me after I left,' she dismissed contemptuously, hardly able to believe he was capable of such vindictiveness. And yet he was here, wasn't he?

'Christi told me nothing——'

'I can't believe that,' she derided scornfully.

Zach gave a heavy sigh. 'No, perhaps that isn't true,' he conceded. 'She did tell me one thing about you. That you have your own reasons for keeping your relationship with Martin Ellington-James and Valerie Sherman secret,' he supplied at her sceptical look. 'And that those reasons had nothing whatsoever to do with the subterfuge she persuaded you to enter into with her.'

'I can't believe that's all she told you about me.' Dizzy shook her head.

'Christi is completely loyal to you, Dizzy,' Zach assured her gently. 'And she assured me your numerous friends, and six godchildren, felt the same way,' he said drily. 'I think at the time I must have still been giving the impression that I would like to put you over my knee and administer the sound beating you obviously missed out on as a child.'

Tears instantly filled her eyes. 'There are other ways to punish a child besides physical violence.'

He frowned, his breath harsh. 'And I want you to tell me all of them,' he urged softly. 'But not before I've told you a few things about myself that might make you feel more like confiding in me,' he added ruefully as she tensed.

Dizzy faced him defensively. 'I doubt there is anything you have to say that would make me feel like that.'

His mouth twisted. 'I know I deserve that, that I should have had more faith in you. But, if it's any consolation, I knew before I had finished sorting things out with Christi that I had been wrong to flare up at you the way I did.'

'Because Christi had explained all the misunder-standings to you——'

'I told you, she told me nothing,' he cut in firmly. 'She reminded me that we all have secrets we find it difficult to confide in other people,' he said flatly.

'Not you.' Dizzy shook her head with certainty.

He gave a deep sigh. 'Especially me,' he grimaced.

Her expression softened. 'If you're talking about your fiancée, and the fact that she died eleven years ago, Christi has already told me about that.' She gave an apologetic shrug.

'Obviously,' Zach drawled. 'But I don't find it difficult to talk about Julie at all.' He shook his head. 'As you said, it was eleven years ago, and although I loved her very much I can't bring her back. My life has gone on, Dizzy,' he spoke softly. 'Progressed. Julie and I perhaps wouldn't have anything in common if we were to meet again now.

Not like you and I do,' he added huskily, his gaze gently caressing.

They had *nothing* in common! Her childhood had emotionally scarred her; the way she lived, her deliberate lack of a place to call home, were a direct result of those scars. Zach had his life all mapped out for him, had a castle for a home, that he obviously loved very much. He was a staid and settled professor—although she had to admit he looked a little less so today, looked younger, too—while she lived like a bohemian. How on earth could he claim they had *anything* in common!

'Dizzy.' Zach's voice was compelling, demanding she look up at him, his expression softly caressing when she finally did so. 'Dizzy, *I'm* Claudia Laurence.'

CHAPTER TEN

D ɪ ᴢ ᴢ ʏ blinked, and blinked again, but he still stood there, looking down at her with rueful apology.

She swallowed hard. 'You—you're——'

'Claudia Laurence,' he repeated heavily. 'Come and sit down,' he took hold of her arm and led her docilely over to the sofa, 'before you fall down!' he added drily, as she still gazed up at him disbelievingly.

She did sit down, heavily, staring up at him. 'Won't——' She cleared her throat as her voice came out a croaky squeak. 'Won't David be wanting his office back?' she finally managed to ask.

Zach shook his head, sitting down beside her, taking her hand in his. 'He told me to take as long as I like to try and sort out the mess I've made of things between us,' he encouraged gently.

'Us?' Dizzy echoed, half fearfully—but oh, so hopefully!

His other hand moved up to caress one of her cheeks in gentle wonder. 'I love you, Dizzy James——'

'Ellington-James,' she corrected harshly, her eyes suddenly full of all the unhappy memories.

Zach settled back on the sofa, pulling her against him, so that her head rested on his shoulder as he caressed her silky hair. 'I have a solution to that, if you would like to hear it?'

She could feel his tension beneath her cheek, knowing he wasn't as relaxed as he would like to appear. She nodded wordlessly, not in the least relaxed herself.

He let out a shaky breath. 'How does Dizzy Bennett sound to you?'

She sat up abruptly, staring down at him, finding only pleading sincerity in his face. She moistened her lips dazedly. Was Zach asking her to *marry* him? Well, he wasn't offering to adopt her, she admonished herself! But marriage? Oh, Christi had joked about it during their stay at Castle Haven, but Dizzy had never actually thought it might happen.

Zach swallowed hard. 'If you find that idea so distasteful that it leaves you speechless, perhaps you would prefer——'

'I don't find the idea of being your wife in the least distasteful!' she burst out in desperate denial. 'I just—you took me by surprise,' she admitted in understatement. 'You don't know anything about me.' She shook her head, sure he couldn't be serious.

'I know that you're completely loyal to those you care about, that you have compassion and love for a child you didn't even know——'

'Kate?' she frowned.

'Kate,' he nodded. 'Mrs Scott was most distressed that you had left before she had had time to thank you properly for all the help you gave her with Kate.'

'Oh,' she grimaced.

'Hmm!' He gave her a reproving look. 'So much for Christi the Good Samaritan!'

'She would have done the same thing if she had found out about Kate first,' Dizzy defended.

'You see,' Zach said with satisfaction, 'completely loyal. Maybe she would,' he conceded as Dizzy still continued to look indignant. 'But she didn't know about Kate first, you did, and you did the only thing someone as loving and lovely as you could do: you did everything within your power to make Kate happy again.'

'Anyone would have done the same,' she said uncomfortably.

'Anyone didn't, you did.' He tapped her reprovingly on the nose for her modesty. 'It's just part of your nature that you didn't want any thanks for what you did.'

'Is that *all* you know about me?' she frowned.

He smiled. 'Isn't it enough?' he teased.

'It doesn't seem an awful lot to base a marriage proposal on.' She still frowned. 'Unless you're just trying to get a Dizzy James illustration free for your next book?' she added lightly, the fact that everything might, just *might*, be going to work out after all, beginning to penetrate the misery she had known the last twenty-four hours.

'I never thought of that,' he said ruefully. 'Will I? As your husband?'

'No,' she mocked.

'As your lover?'

'No.' She began to smile, more and more sure with each passing second that Zach *did* love her, and began to be filled with a rosy glow of love reciprocated.

'As your husband *and* your lover?' he amended hopefully.

'Well...' She began to weaken. 'But you don't *have* to marry me if you would prefer—well, prefer——'

'I know I don't *have* to marry you,' he chided teasingly. 'Even I'm not so old and fusty and dusty that I don't realise you have to indulge in a little more lovemaking than we have so far to produce offspring.'

Colour heightened Dizzy's face at his easy use of the way she and Christi had used to describe him before Dizzy had actually met him. 'Christi told you about those names?' she grimaced.

He nodded, his eyes filled with laughter. 'They were among the few choice ones she chose to call me when she realised I had asked you to leave. And believe me, they were the more polite names she used!'

Dizzy bit her lip, but she couldn't completely stop the smile that formed on her lips. 'Christi is slow to lose her temper, but when she does, watch out!'

'So I discovered,' he grimaced ruefully. 'I concluded that any woman capable of language like that was more than able to take care of herself, and her money!'

Dizzy's eyes lit up with excitement. 'You decided to let her have her inheritance, after all?'

'There was never any doubt about it, Dizzy,' he said gently. 'I told you that yesterday. I had no idea of the interpretation Christi had put on my invitation to come and stay for a few weeks. If I had, I would have disabused her of that conclusion right away. Michael and Diana merely wanted Christi and me to remain close, not to have me test her, like some Victorian uncle.'

'I bet Christi is pleased.' Dizzy settled back against his shoulder.

'Not so that you would notice the last time we spoke,' he admitted ruefully. 'She made it perfectly clear that, if I was too stupid to do anything about my love for you, then she washed her hands of me until I did something about getting you back. This "charade" was supposed to do that, at the same time as showing you I was hiding something, too.'

It thrilled her to hear him talking so naturally about loving her. She wished she could admit the emotion as easily.

'That's sounds a bit strong for Christi,' she frowned at her friend's vehemence.

He gave a rueful sigh. 'I had just told her that I thought I was too old for you, too fusty and dusty, and that maybe you saw me as a father figure, as you didn't seem to be all that close to your own father,' he admitted reluctantly.

'You *what*?' Dizzy moved to glare down at him. 'How dare you——'

'Please,' he held up his hands defensively, wincing dramatically, 'Christi has already made it plain what you would think of that conclusion.'

'I should hope so,' she said indignantly. 'Did I kiss you as if I considered you a father figure, did I *want* you as if I felt that way? Honestly, Zach—is that why you've had your hair styled differently and been out and bought a new suit?' she frowned suspiciously.

He gave a rueful smile. 'I didn't think it would do any harm to smarten myself up a bit. I haven't bothered——'

'Of course it's done some harm,' she scolded. 'I'm probably going to have to beat all the other women off you now that the tailoring of that suit reveals the obvious masculinity of my Greek god! That was my name for you after I saw you swimming naked in the lake that day,' she revealed awkwardly.

'I'm flattered,' Zach grinned, sobering abruptly as he realised what else she had said. 'Does that mean you're going to marry me?' he prompted eagerly.

She swallowed hard. 'I may not be very good at being a wife——'

'You'll be perfect for me,' he said with certainty. 'And just think of the fact that you'll have exclusive rights to all the Claudia Laurence covers from now on,' he tempted.

'Are you really Claudia Laurence?' She looked at him quizzically, unable to envisage him writing those steamy historicals that were so famous worldwide.

Zach gave her a gently reproving look. 'Are you really avoiding giving me an answer?'

Dizzy drew in a ragged breath, her hand moving shakily to the hardness of his cheek. 'Only for the moment,' she admitted. 'Until I've had a chance to get used to the idea of your loving me.' She gave him a pleading look.

Love blazed out of his eyes before he bent his head to kiss the palm of her hand. 'I'll always love you, Dizzy,' he told her gruffly. 'You're the sort of woman a man meets only once in a lifetime, utterly unique. I knew it the moment I first looked at you.'

Just as she had experienced attraction for the first time when she looked at him, had known instinctively that Zach was her one chance at love. She had no doubts that her love for him would ever change, or that she would always want him in a way she had never even dreamt of wanting any other man. It was having him love her in the same way that was so hard to become accustomed to. There were still so many misunderstandings between Zach and herself, and yet now that he was over his own pained humiliation of yesterday she didn't doubt that he loved her unquestioningly. No one had ever loved her like this before; the love of Christi and her other friends was a different sort of love altogether.

'I'm in no rush,' Zach comforted as he saw her bewilderment. 'As long as you don't move further away from me than you are right now while you make your decision,' he added ruefully.

Dizzy gave a shaky laugh. 'I promise!' She snuggled down against him.

'Then, to answer your question,' he said briskly, 'yes, I really am Claudia Laurence.' He sounded a little embarrassed at having to make the admission.

Dizzy frowned, remembering what he had said about Christi reminding him that everyone had secrets they would rather weren't made public. Could this be the answer to the obscure statement Christi had once made about 'knowing' something about her uncle that he wouldn't be too pleased about if he realised she knew? She had a feeling it was.

'Does Christi know?' she asked lightly.

'Oh, yes,' Zach grimaced. 'Apparently she came looking for me in my study one day, and saw some papers I had left lying about on my desk. Also, there was the evidence of my parents' names. Claudia, and Laurence,' he supplied as Dizzy looked at him questioningly. 'Well, how else was I supposed to come up with a pseudonym for a writer of "hot historicals"?' he defended at Dizzy's grin.

'It sounds perfectly logical to me,' she teased.

He sighed. 'I started out writing them because I needed the money—you may have noticed that buying and keeping up a castle doesn't come cheap,' he added self-derisively.

She nodded. 'Christi and I wondered about it several times.'

'No doubt, with the sort of opinion you two young ladies had of me, you decided I'd robbed a bank or something!' he said disgustedly.

'Nothing as shocking as that,' she teased.

'No,' he drawled heavily. 'That would probably have been a little too exciting for the fusty, dusty professor.'

Dizzy put a silencing finger over his lips. 'I only thought of you in that way until I had met you; then I found you *very* exciting!'

His eyes gleamed. 'Have you had long enough to think yet?' he leered.

They were both making a game out of it now, both knowing that she had already made her decision, that she wouldn't be talking to him this way if she hadn't.

'Not quite,' she dismissed haughtily. She shook her head. 'No wonder Christi was so eager to help me get ready earlier to come over here; she knew exactly who she was sending me off to meet when she arranged the appointment and dropped me off in a taxi downstairs.' She chuckled indulgently. 'She was at my studio when my agent rang,' she explained at Zach's puzzlement. 'She took over the conversation with him once it became obvious I was still too upset about yesterday to even attempt to talk to him.'

'Oh, darling——'

'It's already forgotten,' she quickly reassured at his anguished groan, not meaning to remind him of that unhappy time.

'It isn't,' he said grimly. 'But I swear I'll never mistrust you again.'

Dizzy chuckled to ease the tension. 'Some of the answers to the questions you're going to ask are going to take some believing,' she warned.

'I believe them already,' he promised instantly.

She laughed softly. 'Don't be too hasty! As Christi is always reminding me, the illegal gambling one is a little difficult to accept—and she was the one who persuaded the police not to charge me!'

'Illegal——'

'I warned you,' she teased at his astounded expression.

'Yes, but——' He drew in a deeply controlling breath. 'If you say there's a perfectly logical explanation for it, then I believe you.'

'Oh, I didn't say it was logical.' Dizzy shook her head, her eyes shining like twin emeralds. 'Only that I had an explanation.'

Zach closed his eyes, and he was under control again when he reopened them. 'Just tell me one thing,' he said calmly. 'Is that the only occasion Christi stopped you being locked up in prison?'

The laughter deepened in her eyes. 'Yes, that is the only time,' she confirmed, bursting into unrestrained laughter as Zach obviously had difficulty restraining himself from asking any more questions. 'At the time, I had it in mind to forget about a career where I could use my artistic talent, and Christi knew this reporter——'

'—who just happened to be covering a story about illegal gambling,' Zach finished drily.

'There, now that wasn't so difficult, was it?' She had difficulty holding her laughter in check.

Zach muttered under his breath for several seconds, before looking at her reprovingly. 'I won't bother to point out how serious it could have been.'

She sobered. 'No. Are you ready to hear about Henry yet? Or has Christi already told you about him?' It was highly likely that she had, during her own explanations.

'I told you,' he grimaced. 'All Christi did was tell me what an idiot I was for having let you go out of my life.'

'She didn't explain away any of the half-truths and lies she told you?' Dizzy gasped.

He shrugged. 'I already knew you were closer than sisters, that you couldn't be destitute, considering who your parents are. Besides, Christi refused to explain herself, claiming that if I was stupid enough to let you go then I was also stupid enough to hang on to her money no matter what she said to vindicate herself.'

'And you're still going to let her have her money?' Dizzy gasped with incredulous laughter.

He grinned. 'It was almost like being back twenty years ago with my brother. He was very slow to boil, too, but when he did he let you have it with both barrels! Besides, it's Christi's money, not mine, and besides trying to put one over on her not-so-fusty uncle she seems a very sensible person. She has you for a best friend, doesn't she?' he said, as if that settled the whole matter.

'Oh, Zach!' Dizzy threw her arms around his neck, tears streaming down her face as she kissed him with all the love she had inside her.

Zach returned the kiss with a hunger of his own, tasting her again and again, both of them lost in the wonder of their love, oblivious to the gentle knock on the door.

The man who opened the door stared unabashedly at Dizzy James in the arms of his star author. 'I know I said you could have my office for as long as you like,' David Kendrick drawled, when it seemed they weren't even going to come up for air. 'But I do have a publishing company to run,' he mocked as they both turned to him in astonishment, as if they had both completely forgotten they were in *his* office on a sunny afternoon in summer.

As indeed they had. Dizzy looked shyly at Zach's ruffled appearance, his tie slightly off-centre from where her hands had been inside his unbuttoned shirt, and knew that her own face must be flushed, and her hair in wild disarray.

'Thanks, David.' Zach was the one to collect himself first, deftly rebuttoning his shirt. 'But I haven't had an answer to my proposal yet,' he added ruefully.

The other man grinned at him. 'Of course you have.'

Zach turned to her with eyes full of tenderness. 'I have?'

Her smile couldn't have been any wider if she had tried, dazzling both the men in the room. 'You have,' she glowed.

'I'd like to be best man,' David drawled as he moved to sit behind his desk.

'And Christi wants to be our bridesmaid,' Dizzy told Zach with a breathless laugh, hardly able to believe this was really happening.

'Then that seems to be settled, then.' His arm about her shoulders held her tightly to his side, and his face was full of pride as he looked down at her.

'Not quite,' she grimaced. 'I still haven't told you who Henry is.'

'You can tell me on the way to your studio,' he decided firmly. 'Maybe I can also be one of the privileged few who know what DC stands for,' he added teasingly.

'Oh, that's easy——' David broke off as they both turned to him, Dizzy with a silencing frown, Zach with open curiosity. 'It's on her contracts,' he shrugged lamely.

'Talking of contracts, David——' Zach spoke authoritatively, effectively ending the subject of Dizzy's names, knowing she would rather they were alone when they were revealed.

'I know.' David put up defensive hands. 'You want your money as soon as possible so that you can put heating into your castle. I suppose that's only reasonable when you intend taking your bride back there,' he teased. 'Or do you intend generating your own heat?'

Zach's gaze was frankly sensual as he gazed down at Dizzy. 'Oh, I think we'll get by for a while,' he murmured throatily.

Dizzy put her arm through the crook of his. 'More than a while,' she breathed huskily.

'Get out of here, before you set fire to my office!' David complained, grinning widely as they left the room, having eyes only for each other.

Dizzy went with Zach unhesitantly, knowing she could trust him implicitly with her future—and her past.

Zach held her tightly against his side as they walked to the lift. 'I've just remembered something else I learnt about you in the few days I've known you,' he murmured against her ear as the lift doors opened smoothly in front of them.

Dizzy looked up at him with glowing eyes. 'Oh, yes?'

'Yes.' He turned her into his arms, moulding her body against his, a move perfectly in keeping with her Greek god. 'I learnt——' His lips moved against her earlobe. 'I learnt,' he began again, 'that you excite me beyond thinking. There hasn't been a moment go by when I haven't wanted to make love to you. And I know I'm going to feel that way for the rest of my life,' he told her deeply, his gaze holding hers as he told her of his love.

Dizzy flung her arms about his neck. 'I love you!' she groaned emotionally as the lift doors closed behind them to quietly whisk them down to the ground floor.

Her ecstatic statement was followed by a very satisfactory silence, and then the soft murmur of voices, and then Zach's, 'Henry's a *what*?', followed by Dizzy's giggles of pure happiness.

'That young lady needs to be taught a lesson,' Zach stormed as they stepped out of the building to hail a taxi.

Dizzy gave a secretive smile. 'That's just what I've been thinking.'

Zach looked down at her suspiciously. 'What are you up to?' He voiced his reservation.

'Nothing,' she dismissed innocently. 'Yet,' she added softly.

'That's what I was afraid of.' He frowned with the look of a man who had suddenly realised he had his very own 'tiger by the tail'. But the satisfied smile that instantly followed the frown negated any idea that he was dissatisfied with the arrangement; rather, he looked as if he were going to enjoy every moment of the rest of his life. 'Do you think we might have a few months' grace before you start teaching Christi this lesson?' he grimaced.

'Of course!' She looked at him with widely innocent eyes. 'I have the new Claudia Laurence cover to keep me occupied for——'

'You have *me* to keep you occupied,' Zach growled with mock ferocity.

This laughing together was a side of a man and woman together that Dizzy had never experienced. From her memories of them together, her parents had either been arguing or not talking at all, so that the closest she had come to this warm satisfaction of teasing each other had been with her friends. And being like this with Zach was nothing like that.

But all the laughter stopped once they reached her studio. Zach took her in his arms and made such exquisite love to her that tears streamed down her cheeks as they reached total fulfilment together, the moment so poignantly beautiful she never wanted it to end.

Even when that aching pleasure did end, the closeness didn't, and she knew a oneness with Zach that totally engulfed and protected her.

Talking about her parents, her childhood, didn't seem so difficult to do any more, although, as Zach tensed beside her in the narrow bed, she knew he was furiously angry at the suffering her parents had caused her.

She didn't look at him as she told him how her father had never wanted her, how her mother had walked out on them both when she couldn't take any more. She trembled slightly as she remembered how she had been bewildered by her mother's disappearance, pleading with her father to tell her where she had gone. His answer had been to send her to her bedroom without company or food for the rest of the day, the dark shadows of Knollsley Hall taking on frightening proportions to the lonely little girl who cried alone for the mother who hadn't wanted her and the father who couldn't love her.

'The bastard!' Zach rasped fiercely. 'My God, no wonder that painting of Knollsley Hall gave you the shudders! And that little girl in ''Lost Child'' is you, isn't she?' he realised with a pained groan.

Dizzy shook her head. 'I think that would be crediting my mother with feelings she doesn't have. I've always believed the painting was a self-portrait, her way of expressing her own unhappiness with my father, the indulged prison she felt he had locked her into. She has the same colouring as me, you see, even down to this fly-away hair,' she said, attempting to lighten the tension, while Zach's arms gripped her tightly to him.

He stroked her hair tenderly. 'I love your hair.' He kissed the silky softness.

She gave a shaky smile. 'My mother couldn't have cared anything about me, because she never even attempted to see me after she ran away from my father, didn't care that she had left me with the monster she couldn't stand being married to,' she added bitterly.

Zach breathed unevenly beneath her cheek. 'Tell me what else he did to you,' he encouraged tautly.

She did, vividly remembering how she had met the same terrifying fate every time she asked when her mother was coming home, so that in the end she stopped even mentioning her mother, for fear of being sent to the loneliness of the room that was fast becoming her own prison, the dark rooms and corridors of Knollsley Hall becoming a nightmare to her.

Zach held her close as the tears fell softly against her cheeks, and she told him of the fear she still had of darkness, how most nights she read with the light on until she either fell into an exhausted sleep or the dawn began to break.

'You'll never be alone in the darkness again,' he assured her raggedly, kissing the tears from her cheeks. 'And you'll never have to even think of your parents again. Two people like that don't deserve the beauty of a daughter like you!'

She gave a shaky smile, relieved the truth was all told. 'You could be a little biased,' she gently teased him.

He frowned. 'I'm a lot biased,' he agreed firmly. 'I loved you the minute I saw you, and I'll go on loving you until the day I die.'

Dizzy responded with all the warmth there was in her, their lovemaking even more fiery than the first time, all the shadows forgotten as they once again lay replete in each other's arms.

Zach absently played with the wildness of her hair, he was flushed and younger looking, his face softened by love. 'You still haven't told me what DC stands for,' he realised lazily.

All the secrets *hadn't* been revealed! She had completely forgotten the mystery that still surrounded her names.

She leant up on one elbow, bending to whisper softly in Zach's ear.

'Really?' he gasped as she straightened. 'Good lord,' he added dazedly.

Dizzy laughed softly at his reaction, confident she would know nothing but the complete happiness of being loved by Zach for the rest of her life.

Dizzy sat on the grassy slope, watching her husband as he cavorted about in the water, smiling brightly as he saw her there and swam to the shore, gasping breathlessly as he stepped naked from the water.

Almost three months of marriage had given him a relaxed and confident appearance; he moved with a feline grace that never ceased to make Dizzy's heart spin.

He was beautiful, and in that moment she wanted him with a need that bordered on desperation, standing up to slowly begin removing her clothes.

Zach grinned as he helped her with the buttons to her blouse. 'I thought you would never join me,' he murmured appreciatively as he bared her breasts for his enjoyment.

Dizzy's back arched as he drew one sensitised peak into his mouth.

The seclusion of this lake had become their own little paradise, Zach having confided in her that he had discovered the delights of nude bathing while researching the practicality of it for one of his books. Dizzy was more than willing to aid him with all his research now!

It was some time later before she was able to think clearly again. She was nestled snugly on top of Zach's body, their breathing slowly steadying.

She kissed the golden skin of his chest. 'I have some news for you,' she muttered between kisses.

'Hm?' Zach groaned his sleepy satisfaction.

'We're going to have a baby.'

She had known he wouldn't remain sleepy for long after she had made this announcement, and suddenly found herself lying on the blanket at his side as he stared down at her incredulously.

'Don't look so shocked, Zach,' she teased him as he remained speechless. 'It's perfectly natural, after what we've been doing constantly for the last three months,' she told him indulgently.

His stunned gaze moved slowly over the slenderness of her body, lingering on the flatness of her stomach before moving sharply to her face. 'Are you sure?' he breathed raggedly.

She knew the reason for his dazed disbelief: the two of them had made a conscious decision two months ago to try for a baby, but neither of them had expected to be so immediately successful.

'Oh, I'm sure, Zach.' She stretched lazily. 'They taught us in biology at school that——'

'I didn't mean are you sure about *that*,' he reproved impatiently at her teasing smile. 'I meant, are you sure about——' His hand came to rest possessively on the flatness of her stomach.

She made a concerted effort not to laugh with sheer happiness. 'I opened a tin of pilchards for my lunch just now and they made me feel nauseous,' she told him in a deadpan voice.

'You *are* pregnant!' He gave a joyous cry, sweeping her up into his arms, then becoming suddenly still as he looked down at her anxiously. 'Are you all right? Is the baby all right? You shouldn't be lying on this damp grass in your condition!' He hastily began to bundle her back into her clothes.

'I'm fine.' She helped him as best she could, pushing her arms into her blouse, as he seemed intent on strangling her with it. 'The baby is fine. And the grass isn't damp,' she teased indulgently. 'It may be September, but it hasn't rained for weeks.'

'I don't want you catching a chill.' Zach didn't seem to have heard her reassurances, he was so intent on dressing her. 'I'm going to be with you the whole time, you know,' he told her as he zipped her back into her denims. 'No one is going to push me out of the delivery-room just as my daughter is about to be born!' he added firmly.

'We have months to go yet,' she laughed happily. 'And it could be a son,' she warned.

He shook his head. 'A daughter, as beautiful as her mother.'

'But not with such awful names!' Dizzy wrinkled her nose self-disgustedly.

Zach grinned. 'I think one Delilah Cleopatra is enough in any family!'

'Ssh!' She looked about them anxiously.

He laughed at her hunted expression. 'I'll never forget the look on the vicar's face when you asked him if he *had* to read out your full names!'

Dizzy gave him a reproving glance. 'It almost stopped me marrying you!'

'No chance,' he said confidently, taking her into his arms. 'Look at it this way, Dizzy,' he taunted at her outraged expression. 'By marrying me, only a few guests heard your "skeleton in the cupboard". If you had refused to go through with it, the whole world would have known about Delilah Cleopatra when I gave the information to the media!'

'You wouldn't have dared!' Her eyes were wide with indignation.

'Of course I would,' he said without remorse. 'Then you would have had no reason not to marry me.'

'Except that you would have been in hospital in traction,' she frowned fiercely.

He chuckled softly. 'I love it when you get aggressive.'

'Zachariah Bennett——'

'Yes—Dizzy Bennett?' he prompted gently.

She became suddenly still in his arms, her expression softening. 'I *love* you,' she told him breathlessly.

His own laughter faded. 'I love you, too. But then, that's as it should be between two people who are going to spend the rest of their lives living and loving together.'

The rest of their lives...

Yes, she didn't doubt it would be that way between her and Zach.

How lucky she was that the one man she had known she could love was in love with her, too. That 'one chance at love' had been all she needed!

Harlequin *Presents*

Coming Next Month

1119 COMPARATIVE STRANGERS Sara Craven
Nigel's betrayal had shattered Amanda's dreams of their happy life together.
She doesn't know where to turn until Malory, Nigel's elder brother, takes
charge. He's a virtual stranger to her, yet she finds herself agreeing to
marry him!

1120 LOVE IN A MIST Sandra Field
A disastrous early marriage had brought Sally a small daughter she adored but
left her wary about love and commitment. It was ironic that trying to make a
new start on a holiday on St. Pierre she should meet attractive Luke Sheridan.
He felt exactly the same way she did....

1121 HEART OF THE HAWK Sandra Marton
As a step-aunt with skimpy earnings, Rachel has no legal chance of keeping her
nephew when his wealthy father comes to claim him. She discovers why David
Griffin is called The Hawk—and begins to realize the complications facing her.

1122 TRIAL OF INNOCENCE Anne Mather
Throughout her marriage to Stephen Morley, Robyn kept her guilty secret.
And she has no intention of revealing the truth now—even though Stephen is
dead and his brother, Jared, is asking questions that demand answers!

1123 TOO MUCH TO LOSE Susanne McCarthy
Jessica doesn't deserve her reputation as a scarlet woman, but finds it
impossible to set the record straight. Not that she cares what people think,
especially Sam Ryder. She needs him to save her business—that's the only
reason he's in her life.

1124 TAKE THIS WOMAN Lilian Peake
Kirsten is surprised when she inherits her late employer's country mansion.
She's even more surprised to find herself attracted to his great-nephew, Scott
Baird—especially when Scott wants to ruin all her plans and dreams.

1125 IMPOSSIBLE BARGAIN Patricia Wilson
Money is all that matters to Merissa—for the best of reasons. But Julian
Forrest doesn't know them and promptly jumps to all the wrong conclusions
about her. So why should he want her to pose as his fiancée?

1126 SHADOWS ON BALI Karen van der Zee
Nick Donovan broke Megan's heart two years ago when he plainly rejected her.
Now, meeting again, they're forced to work together on the same project in
Bali. And to Megan's disgust, Nick expects her to behave as if nothing had
happened!

Available in November wherever paperback books are sold, or through
Harlequin Reader Service:

In the U.S.
901 Fuhrmann Blvd.
P.O. Box 1397
Buffalo, N.Y. 14240-1397

In Canada
P.O. Box 603
Fort Erie, Ontario
L2A 5X3

Take 4 books & a surprise gift FREE

SPECIAL LIMITED-TIME OFFER

Mail to **Harlequin Reader Service**®

In the U.S.
901 Fuhrmann Blvd.
P.O. Box 1867
Buffalo, N.Y. 14269-1867

In Canada
P.O. Box 609
Fort Erie, Ontario
L2A 5X3

YES! Please send me 4 free Harlequin Temptation® novels and my free surprise gift. Then send me 4 brand-new novels every month as they come off the presses. Bill me at the low price of $2.24 each*—a 10% saving off the retail price. There are no shipping, handling or other hidden costs. There is no minimum number of books I must purchase. I can always return a shipment and cancel at any time. Even if I never buy another book from Harlequin, the 4 free novels and the surprise gift are mine to keep forever.   142 BPX BP7F

*Plus 49¢ postage and handling per shipment in Canada.

Name _____ (PLEASE PRINT)

Address _____ Apt. No. _____

City _____ State/Prov. _____ Zip/Postal Code _____

This offer is limited to one order per household and not valid to present subscribers. Price is subject to change.   DOHT-SUB-1C

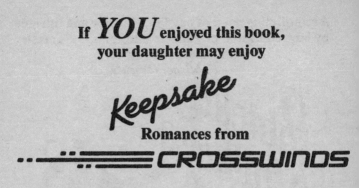

🔷 *Harlequin Superromance*

**Here are the longer, more involving stories you
have been waiting for...Superromance.**

Modern, believable novels of love, full of the complex
joys and heartaches of real people.

Intriguing conflicts based on today's constantly
changing life-styles.

Four new titles every month.
Available wherever paperbacks are sold.